P9-CRR-643

"I am not going to have sex with you..."

There. Kim had said it. Now they could sleep. Even if they were sharing the same king-size bed.

"Sweetheart, forget about sex. I'd be happy if you would just share some of the sheet," Stuart teased.

Kim knew that if she turned to look at him she would see a most excellent male body wearing nothing but silk boxer shorts.

"I usually sleep naked," he had explained earlier. "I bought these to impress you."

She gazed into his dark chocolate eyes. "It will take more than that."

"I can take them off," he murmured.

At her pointed look, he said, "Okay, I shouldn't be lusting after the baby-sitter."

Kim smiled in the darkness. "Do not call me the baby-sitter, as if I'm some teen earning money to spend at the mall."

"All right. You're the sexy photographer accompanying the heart surgeon to Maine. We're about to have a sexual encounter in a romantic, historic inn while the baby sleeps like a log and doesn't wake up till nine the next morning."

Maybe I am going to have sex with you....

Dear Reader,

Welcome to the Cooper family! Vicki Lewis Thompson, Jill Shalvis and I have the good fortune to introduce a new Harlequin continuity series by bringing you stories about Kim, Kate and Nick Cooper—the Rhode Island branch of the Cooper's Corner family. Charles Cooper sired twin sons, John and Justin, before dying in World War II. John grew up with a camera in his hand and talent for photography that led to a newspaper job and his own studio in Rhode Island.

Kim and Kate, John's twins, run the family's photography business after their parents retire to Florida. When shy Kim meets Stuart Thorpe, little does she know she's about to hit the road with a baby and the man of her dreams. So, of course, sister Kate will have a wedding to plan, while trying to stay out of bed with the best man. And then there's older brother Nick, an adventurer looking for peace and quiet only to discover he's hiding a mysterious woman and her large dog.

The day after I finished this book, my husband and I took off for Plymouth to visit the "rock" and enjoy a gorgeous autumn day. We followed Kim and Stuart's trail and, like this story's characters, promptly became lost outside Boston. We've also been lost in Salem, Providence, Concord and New Haven, so there's a pattern here!

I hope you enjoy our branch of the Cooper clan. And please visit New England. Order a lobster roll. Spend a romantic night at a bed-and-breakfast—maybe in the town of Cooper's Corner. But please don't forget to buy a map.

Happy reading!

Kristine Rolofson

Kristine Rolofson
THE BABY
AND THE BACHELOR

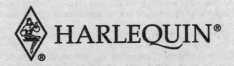

HARLEQUIN®

TORONTO • NEW YORK • LONDON
AMSTERDAM • PARIS • SYDNEY • HAMBURG
STOCKHOLM • ATHENS • TOKYO • MILAN • MADRID
PRAGUE • WARSAW • BUDAPEST • AUCKLAND

If you purchased this book without a cover you should be aware
that this book is stolen property. It was reported as "unsold and
destroyed" to the publisher, and neither the author nor the
publisher has received any payment for this "stripped book."

ISBN 0-373-25977-8

THE BABY AND THE BACHELOR

Copyright © 2002 by Harlequin Books S.A.

Kristine Rolofson is acknowledged as the author of this work.

All rights reserved. Except for use in any review, the reproduction or
utilization of this work in whole or in part in any form by any electronic,
mechanical or other means, now known or hereafter invented, including
xerography, photocopying and recording, or in any information storage
or retrieval system, is forbidden without the written permission of the
publisher, Harlequin Enterprises Limited, 225 Duncan Mill Road,
Don Mills, Ontario, Canada M3B 3K9.

All characters in this book have no existence outside the imagination of
the author and have no relation whatsoever to anyone bearing the same
name or names. They are not even distantly inspired by any individual
known or unknown to the author, and all incidents are pure invention.

This edition published by arrangement with Harlequin Books S.A.

® and TM are trademarks of the publisher. Trademarks indicated with
® are registered in the United States Patent and Trademark Office, the
Canadian Trade Marks Office and in other countries.

Visit us at www.eHarlequin.com

Printed in U.S.A.

1

"I GOT YOU OUT OF BED? That figures."

"Payne, I worked until five-thirty this morning." Stuart Thorpe, dressed in his oldest T-shirt and khaki shorts, took the baby from his sister's arms and watched Payne dump an armload of baby paraphernalia on his marble-tiled floor. "I'm relaxing. What do you think I'm doing on my day off?"

"Having orgies, wild parties, and other sorts of things I won't mention," she answered, giving him that disapproving older sister look he was very familiar with, having experienced it for all of his thirty-five years.

"My college memories are very important to me," he teased, since Payne knew full well that he had worked too many hours studying to spend time on parties of any kind.

"You don't have a woman asleep in there, do you?"

"No." His sisters tended to exaggerate the extent of his social life, only because he hadn't settled down yet, something that seemed to worry both of them. "Bambi left early to go to work at the Foxy Lady."

Payne glared at him. "I never know if you're joking or not. Isn't the Foxy Lady that place where exotic dancers serve breakfast?"

"Yes, it is and yes, I'm joking. I swear. I haven't been to the Foxy Lady since my twenty-first birthday."

"You don't need to," she muttered, moving past him to deposit a fistful of bottles in his refrigerator. "Women throw themselves at you all the time. It's ridiculous."

"I think it's nice." He grinned at his niece, whose chubby fingers patted his cheek. "Uncle Stuart has lots of very pretty friends."

"Well," Payne said. "Keep your pretty friends away while Bree is here. I don't want you distracted from baby-sitting."

"Sure." Stuart would have laughed, but he didn't dare. He kept his family and his social life separate, so whatever lovely lady he was dating wouldn't get the wrong idea and think there was going to be anything permanent in the future. Payne didn't look the least bit relieved, but she couldn't take the baby to Maine with her either, not right now.

"Do you really think you can handle this until Temple gets home?" she asked. Temple was their younger sister.

"No problem," Stuart uttered, but he knew and his sister knew that taking care of a six-month-old baby was one hell of a job and not under the "no problem" category at all. But Stuart figured he and Bree could muddle through. "What's an uncle for?"

"Are you sure?" Payne looked worried, but his older sister almost always looked worried. Stuart moved her toward the door.

"We'll get along just fine." His niece was in his arms, tugging on his earlobe as if she wanted to remove it from his head and fling it across the polished wood floor. Brianne Nicole Johnson liked to throw all sorts of things. "You brought her playpen, right?"

"It's outside, by the door." She paused and looked around his black-and-white living room. "This ultramodern furniture looks dangerous."

He looked at his glass and chrome coffee table, his leather sofa and an entertainment center that had cost more than a semester at college. "It costs too much to be dangerous and besides, Bree is going to be too busy to have time to hurt herself, Payne. The activities list you gave me is two pages long."

His oldest sister frowned again, but this time she walked toward the door. "Temple will be back in town by dinnertime. She said she'd call you from the airport and then come right over and get Bree."

"Fine. Give me a call tonight and let me know how Phil's mother is."

"I will." Now Payne looked as if she was about to cry. She loved her in-laws, and the thought of her mother-in-law in the hospital was almost more than Payne could bear, especially now, with her husband in Australia on a business trip. The three Thorpe siblings shared the same dark hair, athletic builds and dark brown eyes, but Payne was the emotional one of the family. And, as the oldest, the bossiest. "Make sure she eats on time."

"Mummm," the baby hummed, one chubby hand reaching out to her mother. Payne kissed her three more times and then hurried toward the door. She turned around once more and gave her brother another order. "You will make sure she takes a nap? And that her car seat is fastened correctly? And if she gets sick or anything, you can call her pediatrician. The number's in the bag."

"Fine."

"And tell Temple I'm counting on her."

"We can take care of Bree," he assured her, knowing damn well his sisters didn't actually believe he was thirty-five.

"Don't forget her photo appointment at four-thirty. If she doesn't get it done now I'll have to wait another three months to get in. Oh, and I scheduled it between her nap and her dinner, so make sure you follow the schedule," was Payne's parting order.

"Will do." Stuart shut the door and turned to Bree. "Your mom's a real pain in the—well, you'll figure that out when you're fifteen." Bree's big brown eyes stared unblinking at him. "Then you call Uncle Stuart for help, okay?"

"Mmmm," his niece gurgled and gave his ear another painful twist.

Stuart glanced at the clock on the mantel. It was going to be a long afternoon.

"I JUST DON'T KNOW WHERE the time goes," Anna Gianetto muttered. She squinted at her watch. "Is it four-thirty or three-thirty?"

"Four-thirty," Kim told her neighbor.

"Already? Ooh," she said, fanning her ample bosom with a Providence Photography brochure. "I brought you too many things today."

"It's okay. My last appointment isn't here yet." Kim adjusted the array of children's clothes so that the light was right and then, with Anna's digital camera, took the picture.

"You do good work," Pat O'Reilly said, patting Kim on the back while Anna retrieved the clothing. "You're a good girl to do this for us."

"I don't mind," she told them. She knew they were worried about her right now. Everyone was, which was more than a little disconcerting. Kim Cooper never liked being the center of attention.

"Well, you're a good girl," Patrick repeated.

"I know." She winked at him. Her neighbors were like family since she'd known them almost all her life. Their venture into selling things on eBay, an online auction house, provided them with extra spending money and Kim with their company. They made her laugh, though her sister Kate thought Kim was a little bit crazy for hanging out with the elderly neighbors. "It's a nice change from babies and cats and dogs."

Patrick, a short, wiry man in his early eighties, shook one gnarled finger at her. "One of these days you'll have your own babies, Kimmy, don't you worry."

"I'm not worried," she promised. Two years ago, when Jeff broke off their engagement and said he "couldn't commit," she'd believed her family's declarations that life held all sorts of wonderful surprises and all she had to do was stay cheerful. Recently she'd decided that maybe her life was simply going to be one long day after another. The men her sister had tried to fix her up with hadn't been the least bit interesting—or maybe, to be fair, the men themselves weren't interested in a nonglamorous version of her twin.

"You should get out more," Anna said. "You spend too much time by yourself."

"I will," she promised, as she did every time her neighbors came to the studio. "I promise."

"Robbie likes you," Anna said. "He stops by from that gym of his sometimes, you know. 'Aunt Anny,' he says, 'what am I doin' wrong that Kim won't marry me?'"

"I'm not in love with him, Anna." Kim secretly thought Robbie, a competitive weight lifter, was more in love with his own body than wanting anything to do with hers. Anna, determined to take care of her young neighbor, had a legion of nephews she'd thought were "just right" for Kim.

"You could try harder. Women shouldn't wait so long to get married these days," Anna advised. She put the carefully folded clothing into a brown shopping bag. "That's why they have trouble having babies, now. Their eggs are old. That's not the way it was in our day. I got pregnant on our honeymoon."

"Yeah," Pat said. "Mary and I had our first boy when we were twenty." He frowned, trying to remember. "Or maybe it was nineteen. My memory sure as heck isn't what it used to be."

"It's too bad that things are different now," Kim said, hoping her own eggs would give her a few more optimistic years before drying up. She was only twenty-six, not exactly middle-aged, so shouldn't those little suckers be thriving? "Maybe I'm not the marrying kind."

"Nonsense," Pat said.

"Give me the old days," Anna said. "When men were men."

"And women were women," Patrick added with a sigh. Kim often wished she could have seen what he looked like when he was younger.

She suspected he'd been as handsome as sin and twice as charming. "No one even bakes anymore."

"Hey," Anna said. "You come by and I'll make anise cookies for you."

"Me, too?" Kim had a weakness for her neighbor's Italian specialty.

"Sure, honey. We'll have ourselves a little party," Anna declared, satisfied that she had stuffed everything into her shopping bag.

"We'd better get out of here, Anna." Pat jerked his thumb in the direction of the reception area. "Kimmy has real work to do now."

They all looked toward the open door and heard a baby fussing and a low male voice trying to soothe—Kim searched her memory—Brianne Johnson.

"Hello?" the man called, sounding a little flustered. It was unusual for a father to arrive for a baby's first photo. She hoped Brianne's mother was out there, too, so the little girl would calm down.

"Coming!" Kim hurried over toward the door, a welcoming smile on her face. Her specialty was babies, while Kate did the glamour shots and more artistic projects. And this baby, she saw, was especially gorgeous. She had dark curling hair and big brown eyes, and a dimple in her left cheek when she stopped fussing and smiled at Kim.

"How did you do that?" the father said, and that's when Kim's gaze lifted to the man's face. His very familiar face. At first she didn't think she believed what her brain was trying to tell her: Stuart Thorpe was standing eight feet away.

"Do that?" she echoed, her mind blank except for one thought: Stuart Thorpe was holding a baby.

"Kim?" he said, his beautiful mouth turning into a smile. "Kim Cooper?"

"Yes," she managed to gulp. He would never in a thousand lifetimes mistake her for her twin, of course. No one ever had, not since they were in elementary school. She made an attempt to brush her hair back with her hand and then gave up. Stuart Thorpe still wouldn't notice her unless she was blond, busty and running her hands over his chest—none of which was likely.

"It's been a long time," Stuart said, adjusting his grip on the baby so she wouldn't wriggle out of his arms.

"Years," she agreed. He looked as handsome as ever, she noted with some disappointment.

He hadn't lost any of that thick dark hair. He hadn't gotten fat. He still looked good in anything he wore, even a rumpled polo shirt and shorts that looked as if Brianne had spilled six or seven spoonfuls of baby food on them.

"Five or six years, at least," he repeated, looking dazed. "How are you? And your sister Kate?"

"We're both fine."

"You haven't changed a bit," Stuart said, which wasn't the most flattering thing he could say. Kim knew she had been an awkward, innocent and terribly shy art student with a passion for photography and a secret crush on a young doctor in the apartment downstairs. And she hadn't changed much either, obviously.

"So," she said, trying to regain some resemblance of professionalism. "Let's get Brianne settled in the studio so that she's comfortable. Your wife said she wanted an assortment of pictures to choose from and—"

"Oh," he said, following her into the next room where Anna and Patrick waited, transfixed with curiosity. "That wasn't my wife. You talked to—"

"What a beautiful baby," Anna interrupted, holding out her arms. Brianne, obviously sensing a more comfortable chest to snuggle against, went willingly into Anna's embrace as the plump woman settled herself on Kim's leather sofa.

"Thanks," Stuart said. "She takes after my side of the family, I think."

So he wasn't married to the baby's mother. Divorced? Kim eyed the baby, who wasn't more than five or six months old. No. It was more likely that Stuart and Brianne's mother had never married. No surprise there. Stuart Thorpe attracted women like her twin sister attracted men.

It was a gift.

"Mrs. Gianetto, this is Stuart Thorpe, an old friend. Stuart, this is Anna Gianetto and Patrick O'Reilly, my neighbors."

Patrick frowned at the younger man, but he stepped forward to shake Stuart's offered hand. "Nice to meet you," he said, not sounding as if he meant it. "You know our Kim, huh?"

"Yes."

"She's a nice girl," the old man declared. "A *good* girl."

"Stuart," Kim said quickly. "I heard that you're a heart surgeon now."

"Uh, yes—" he stopped, watching his baby. "Uh, Mrs.—"

"Gianetto," Kim supplied, watching Anna cradle the child.

"Mrs. Gianetto," Stuart tried again. "If you hold her like that she'll think she's going to get fed and then I'm afraid she'll—"

Scream.

Kim winced. Brianne's wail of frustration bounced off the ivory walls of the studio and effectively stopped conversation. Patrick winced and reached for his hearing aid.

"*Mamma mia*," Anna exhaled. "This one has a temper like my first husband." She lifted the little girl and aimed her toward Stuart.

"She takes after her mother," he said, looking amused as he took the baby back into his arms. His smile faded as Brianne's wails escalated.

"Where *is* her mother?" Kim asked.

"In Maine," he shouted. "Family emergency!"

"Maybe it would be better if you waited until her mother returns," Kim suggested. "Your little girl might be in a better mood for her pictures then."

"I'll catch hell for messing this up," he muttered, awkwardly patting the baby's back.

"Can't you do something? Some photographer tricks?"

"Give her to me." She held out her arms and Stuart quickly handed over the baby. Brianne let out one more complaint and then stared at Kim as if she was trying to decide whether to scream again or not.

Patrick glared at Stuart again. "That baby of yours doesn't seem to like her daddy very much."

Stuart ignored him and looked at Kim. "Can you do anything with her? There are some extra clothes in her bag, I think, if we need them. And her blanket."

"Look, sweetheart," Kim said, keeping her voice low. "Would you like to see some pretty toys? Or some funny puppets?" Brianne's brown eyes didn't blink, but she took a deep shuddering breath.

Kim looked over at her audience of three. Stuart appeared relieved and tired. Anna sat on the couch as if she was watching a particularly fascinating television show and Patrick stood with his arms folded across his chest, clearly convinced he was protecting his women from a dangerous stranger.

"I take it you're all staying?" she asked.

"I can wait outside," Stuart offered, taking a step backward.

"Good idea," Patrick said.

"But she knows you," Kim told Stuart. As much as she wished he would leave, she couldn't risk Brianne throwing another fit if she discovered she was alone with strangers. Babies were sensitive little beings, she knew. And they knew what was going on around them.

"If you insist," Stuart said.

"Fine." She didn't want to insist. She wanted her heart to beat normally again and she wanted to stop worrying that her face was red. She also didn't know how much longer she could hide how nervous she was.

"I'll stay, too." Patrick moved over to the couch and sat beside Anna.

"Great," Kim muttered, moving over to the staged area where she photographed children. "You all have to be quiet. I don't want her to be distracted." She turned back to Stuart. "Did you bring any of her favorite toys?"

"I'll look." He practically ran out the door to the waiting room.

"What a nice young man," Anna said. "You were friends, eh? What kind of friends?"

Kim shook her head. "Never mind about

that, Anna. It was a long time ago. I was a senior in art school and he was in residency at Rhode Island Hospital. We lived in the same apartment house in East Providence." She wondered if Brianne would be happier if she was propped into a sitting position or if she would be better on her tummy, lifting her head and smiling for the camera. She would have to try it both ways and hope the little girl wouldn't object too loudly.

"Hmm," her neighbor said. "You must have liked him. I can tell."

"No," Kim said. "Not really." A secret crush, that was all, which she would never admit to anyone. Of course, Stuart hadn't given her a second look after one casual date, except to ask who her twin was dating.

"Humph," was all Anna said as Stuart, holding a pink terry cloth turtle and a darker rose blanket, hurried back into the room. He looked ridiculous and also terribly appealing, Kim thought, hoping she didn't appear too pathetic and wistful as she watched him cross the room.

Funny that the man who swore he'd never settle down was now a father.

HE'D FORGOTTEN Kim Cooper was a photographer—or maybe he never knew. He hadn't forgotten that reddish-gold hair or jade-green eyes or her slender little body. Kim Cooper had had a great-looking ass and still did, despite the fact that she wore baggy shorts. Stuart watched her work with his moody little niece, coaxing the baby into smiling for the camera. He caught the outline of her breasts when she bent over to adjust a black cord, glimpsed a bit of appealing cleavage in the V of her white blouse.

Stuart glanced over at Mr. O'Reilly and hoped the old man couldn't read his mind. Patrick reminded him of an old bulldog his friend Harry had owned years ago.

He turned his attention back to Kim, who now held the baby's toy turtle in the air, coaxing Bree into a smile as she clicked another picture.

"Good girl," Kim cooed and Stuart swore the baby preened.

"What a little sweetheart," the Italian woman declared. "She likes having her picture taken, doesn't she."

"What about a different outfit?" Kim scooped the baby into her arms and turned and looked at Stuart. "Your—Bree's mother wanted quite a lot of proofs from which to choose."

"I don't have a clue." Stuart wondered if he should apologize for not calling Kim, but that seemed silly since six years had passed since their one and only date.

"She didn't tell you?"

He reached in his pants pocket and pulled out a folded piece of yellow-lined paper. "She wrote it down." Stuart unfolded the list and noted that he'd forgotten to call off the "Baby and Me" exercise class, something so important that Payne had starred it. Nap, pink turtle, four-thirty appointment, pink outfit with white bunny and white dress with lace. He looked over at Brianne, who was dressed in a pink one-piece outfit with a teddy bear on the front. "I think I might have a fancy dress," he said.

"Do you want to put it on her while I change the film?"

"Sure." Before he knew it the baby was back in his arms and Kim was immersed in sorting through a strange array of equipment.

He'd forgotten how pretty Kim Cooper was. He didn't see a wedding ring on her left hand, though he sneaked a peek before he went back into the waiting room to fetch the diaper bag. No diamond either, which surprised him. Kim had been the "marriage and babies" kind of woman he'd learned to avoid. Sweet, domestic, innocent, she had been perfect "wife" material.

For someone else.

Which meant he had run like hell in the opposite direction.

Stuart grabbed the baby's bag, stuffed full of her belongings and headed back to the studio.

"We'll do some outdoor pictures now," Kim said, glancing out the window at the bright May sunshine.

"Outside?" Payne hadn't said anything about that. If Bree got stung by a bee, his ass was grass and he'd never be invited to another one of his sister's holiday meals again.

"I have it all set up," she said, doing something with her camera. "The lilacs are going to bloom early this year. If we're lucky we might be able to get a touch of color. At least we'll get some background texture from the bushes, and the light should be good."

"Our Kim is famous for her lilac pictures," Anna confided to Stuart, who thought about ants, bees and ticks. Rhode Island was famous for mosquitoes, too. He rummaged through the bag for Bree's sweater.

"Don't worry about shoes," Kim told him. "She can go barefoot. Baby toes are wonderful."

"They are?"

"They are," she said, pointing to the place on the couch that Mr. O'Reilly had just vacated. "You can change her there. And check her diaper, too. If she's uncomfortable, she's not going to smile."

He did as he was told, laying Bree on her back on the sofa cushion. "Are you sure this outside is a good idea?"

"Trust me," she said, giving him a quick smile that had a strange effect on the part of his body that had no business coming to life at this particular moment, in front of this particular audience.

2

BRIANNE HOWLED HER objections at having her pink outfit removed. She screamed about having her diaper changed. And she made Kim's ears ring when she loudly protested having to put on a new dress.

"Sorry," Stuart muttered, while Anna made the sign of the cross and Patrick once again reached for his hearing aid.

"Maybe I can help." Kim finally put down her camera and took over the care of the child, not that she had much experience in dressing babies. But a blotchy, teary-eyed child would not take a good picture. The little girl knew enough to stick out her lower lip and give Kim a pitiful look from her big brown eyes, so Kim tickled her toes and made her giggle.

"How did you do that?" Stuart stood next to the couch, but out of the baby's sight, as if he was afraid that Brianne would yell at him again.

"I have all sorts of ways to make babies

smile," she said, lifting the little girl into her arms. "Peekaboo, tickles with a feather duster, squeaky toys, things like that."

She gathered the props she needed, handing them to Stuart to carry while she took the baby, who had now stopped crying and looked more curious than anything else. Kim's audience followed her outside and around the side of the house to the backyard.

The lilac garden, a secluded rectangle of lawn bordered two sides by thick lilac bushes, lay behind the next door neighbor's house. The huge white Victorian was the largest house in the neighborhood, and while some of the homes closest to the business-zoned street one block away had converted to businesses, "Lilac House"—with its dark purple shutters and elegant front porch—remained unchanged, as had Patrick's and Anna's large homes across the street.

Until now, Kim thought, ignoring the new No Trespassing sign posted on the whitewashed gate. She'd rented the space from Mr. and Mrs. Carlisle for the past four years, using the area for her outdoor photographs. When Mrs. Carlisle died and her husband went to live with his son, Kim and Kate tried to buy the strip of garden, but their letters to sweet old Mr. Carlisle had gone unanswered. There was little backyard space on their own property; between the garage and the parking area, there was no room to plant lilac bushes.

"Just a shame," Anna muttered, following close behind Kim. "It's so pretty back here and you've gone to so much work."

"What's a shame?" Stuart paused by the wicker baby stroller and frowned down at it. He negotiated his way around Kim's favorite rusted wrought iron table and ornate iron chair, then stepped over several big pots of tulips and hyacinths leftover from the Easter photo sessions.

"That Kimmy can't buy this," the woman explained. "We think the house has been sold and it's going to be turned into apartments and the lilac trees cut down for parking spaces."

"That's just a rumor." Patrick gave Kim a reassuring look. "No one's heard anything for sure."

"I can't seem to find out what's going on," Kim admitted. "Maybe Mr. Carlisle's son is the one in charge of the property now."

"He should be ashamed of himself," Anna

said. "He could have sold you the lilacs after you took care of them all these years."

"It's his property. He can do what he wants." She handed the baby to Anna and then took the vintage sheets from Stuart, who gave her a pleading look.

"Tell me she won't get stung by any flying insects."

"She won't get stung by any flying insects," she repeated obediently, but her attention was focused on arranging the lace-edged sheet so that the wicker would show, too. She intended to take some black-and-white shots, along with the color.

"And we won't be out here long," he added.

"I'll be as fast as I can be," she promised. "If you would all stand back out of the way—no, over there, where you don't cast shadows—Brianne and I will get to work." Not that it would be easy to work, with Stuart frowning at her with that protective look on his face. His vigilance was surprisingly sexy, Kim realized, until she reminded herself to keep her mind on her work. She had no business thinking Stuart Thorpe was sexy, not when she should be concentrating on the job in front of her.

It didn't take long to pose the baby in the

stroller. The pretty little girl appeared to like being outdoors in the warm spring air. Most of the children she photographed did, especially if their feet were bare. Kim took some close-ups of those feet. The onlookers kept silent, except once when Stuart swore at a bee who dared come within eight feet of the wicker stroller.

Then Brianne screamed, spit up carrots on her eyelet lace collar and proceeded to call an end to the photo session.

"I guess that's that," Stuart said with a sigh, lifting her from the stroller. Since he already had carrot stains on his shirt, he didn't seem to mind the new ones.

"I'm sure I have enough for you and her mother to choose from," Kim assured him. Was she one of those socialites she'd seen him with on the front page of the Arts section in the Sunday paper? Was she slim and blond and very rich, with her very own lilacs and a car that didn't need repairs every three months?

"Ooh, I'd like to see those pictures myself," Mrs. G. said. She piled the sheets in her arms and Patrick moved the stroller out of the garden area and onto the back porch, while Kim led Stuart to the front of the house and the studio door.

"You have a lot of help here," Stuart said. "Does Kate work here, too?"

"Yes. She specializes in bridal portraits and graduation photos."

"Not baby toes?"

"No." Kim smiled, remembering her twin's disastrous attempts at photographing a set of triplets last year. "Kate's not exactly the domestic type."

"And her sister?"

She turned and ushered him into the reception room. "Babies are my business."

"Hold her for a minute, will you?" Stuart didn't wait for an answer and Kim found herself cuddling Brianne again while Stuart gathered up the baby's possessions and haphazardly stuffed them into the diaper bag. When they were ready to leave, Kim tweaked Brianne's big toe and made her smile. "Take good care of your daddy, sweetheart. I think he could use a break."

"I'm not her father, if that's what you mean," he said. "She's my niece."

"Whether she's your niece or your daughter, you're still taking care of her, right?" His *niece*? It made more sense, come to think of it. The brilliant and handsome Dr. Thorpe would certainly practice safe sex and birth control. She rubbed the child's little feet with gentle motions. The exhausted baby leaned against her and sighed.

"Yeah, I'm the baby-sitter until her aunt arrives." He looked at his watch and then back to Kim. "Which is any minute now."

"Your *niece?*" Pat looked from Stuart to the baby and then back again. "Why didn't you say that in the first place?"

"I thought I did," he said, shrugging. "My sister's mother-in-law is in intensive care up in Maine. She had to leave before my other sister—the real baby-sitter—got back from vacation."

"She couldn't take the baby?" Kim was surprised.

He shook his head. "There's no other family up there—her husband is on his way home from Sydney—and Payne didn't want to leave her with strangers while she was at the hospital."

"Hospitals are no places for babies," Anna declared. "Too many germs in the waiting rooms, if you know what I mean."

"I'm sure my sister would agree with you," Stuart said.

"Stuart's a doctor, Anna," she reminded her. "He knows all about germs."

"Well, then, he can tell me what this is." Anna pointed to her left arm. "Come here, young man, and see if you know your business and can tell me what this spot is."

"I'm a surgeon, not a dermatologist, but I can tell you if it's chicken pox," Stuart said, but he obeyed the woman and crossed the room to peer at her forearm. "It looks like a wart to me."

"Not skin cancer?"

"I doubt that very much, Mrs. Gianetto, but I can give you the name of a good dermatologist if you want to have it checked further."

"Nah," she said. "I trust you." She stood and reached for her shopping bag.

"Maybe you should do as he says, Anna," Patrick said.

She laughed. "I just saved fifty dollars. Come on, Pat. Let's go back to my house and get these things listed on eBay before we run out of energy."

"Don't forget the camera," Kim said. Patrick picked up the camera and took the shopping bag from Anna's hand.

"Are you closing up?" he asked, clearly unhappy about leaving her alone with a strange man.

"Absolutely," she promised as Anna stopped to pat the baby's head. "Brianne was my last appointment for the day."

"You come for dinner tonight," Anna whispered. "I'll fry up some sausage and peppers just the way you like. And I got some good bread at Zachinini's this morning, too, when I went down to the post office."

"I can't," Kim said, genuinely sorry to miss eating anything from Zachinini's bakery or Anna's kitchen, but the knowing sympathy in her neighbor's expression was more than she could bear. "I've got a lot of work to do. Kate's behind on three weddings—"

"Oh, that one," Anna sighed, rolling her eyes. "She'll be zooming up the street in that fast little car of hers tonight?"

"As far as I know." Kate had called four times today already, unusual for a Friday night, but typical of her protective twin.

"Thanks again, Kimmy," Anna said. "You doing the yard sales with us tomorrow?"

"Maybe." Memorial Day weekend was the unofficial beginning of the yard sale season, which meant an early morning on Saturday looking for "treasures." She knew her neighbors were simply trying to keep her from remembering what she would have been doing this weekend, if things had turned out differently.

"I'll bring the truck," Patrick promised. "We'll go out to breakfast after."

"I'll let you know," Kim said, watching her friends leave. Patrick gave Stuart one last warning look and then went out the door.

"Watch yourself on the steps, Anna," she heard the old man say before the door shut. Kim turned toward Stuart, who gave her a devastating smile.

"Thanks for the help calming her down," he said. "She hasn't closed her eyes since I've had her."

"She's very sweet," Kim said. "I think you'd better take her home and put her to bed."

"You wouldn't want to go home with us, would you? She looks pretty comfortable in your arms."

"I think you can handle it," she said. It really wasn't fair for a man to be that good-looking.

"Tell Brianne that," he said. He stepped closer and, with a gentle motion, lifted the baby and turned her to lean against his food-stained shirt. His fingers grazed Kim's breasts, something she tried to pretend she hadn't felt. "Well, it was good seeing you again."

"You, too. Good luck."

"Tell your sister I said hello."

She looked at Brianne drooling on Stuart's shoulder and smiled. Babies were her favorite clients—and the most challenging.

"Are you sure you won't come home with me?" He had a decidedly wicked and desperate expression, she noticed. He made her want to smile, but she resisted. She knew when she was out of her league, baby or no baby.

"Thanks, but no thanks."

"Too bad." He picked up the diaper bag and the rose blanket in his left hand. "Bree likes you."

"Bye." She took one more longing look at the baby. Cuddling Brianne had been the brightest spot in her day.

"I DON'T LIKE THIS," Patrick declared, sitting down at Anna's kitchen table. He liked Anna's kitchen, because it reminded him of his own, with its faded linoleum floor and solid red and white Formica kitchen set. And Anna's kitchen smelled of food, while his just…smelled. He ate too much popcorn now that he'd figured out the microwave oven his daughter had given him for Christmas last year.

"Don't like what?" Anna's bulk was hidden by the refrigerator door as she removed pan after pan of Italian concoctions. "Hey, you want a beer?"

"I don't like leaving Kimmy with that man," he grumbled, taking the bottle of Budweiser Anna handed him. "Thanks."

"He's a doctor," she reminded him. She lifted the lid off a frying pan and sniffed. "A man of science."

"He's not good enough for her." The twist-off cap popped off easily and Pat took a healthy swallow. His own doctor had told him that one beer a day couldn't hurt anything, not at his age. But Dr. Shaunnesy was pushing sixty, still smoked cigars and visited Ireland once a year. He wasn't some pretty-face, fancy-ass surgeon who wouldn't know good beer if it was poured on his Mercedes.

And Pat had noticed the Mercedes, all right, shiny as could be in the parking area north of Kim Cooper's house. "Give me a Cadillac any day," he said.

"What's cars got to do with anything?" She

arranged all sorts of pans on top of the stove and then took the cork out of a bottle of red wine. She drank a glass every night with dinner, Anna did. And had, she'd informed him once, since she was fifteen.

"I dunno. Can't you do anything with that nephew of yours?"

"Robbie?" She turned from the stove and shrugged. "He says he's asked her to marry him four times and she keeps saying no."

Robbie Gianetto wasn't the brightest light on the porch, in Pat's opinion, but Kimmy was too young to keep grieving like this. Any port in a storm, he figured. Even as shallow a port as Anna's thickheaded nephew. "She needs to get on with her life since things didn't work out with Jeff."

"Look who's talking," Anna said, shaking a wooden spoon at him. "Mary's been gone five years now and you won't even get on a plane and visit your sister."

"I get out of the house enough," he said. "I don't have to fly to California to prove anything. I like my house just fine."

"Humph." Anna stirred the peppers in the pan, filling the kitchen with the aroma of good Italian cooking. "I like my house, too, but at least I get to Florida a couple of times a year to visit my sister and her son."

"I don't think much of Florida," he declared, his stomach rumbling with anticipation. "And I don't think much of that doctor fella either. He's not good enough for Kimmy."

"Somebody better be," Anna said, waving the smoke away from her face. "She's not getting any younger."

"None of us are, Anna," he said, taking another sip of ice-cold beer. "None of us are."

"YOU'RE KIDDING. THE GORGEOUS Stuart Thorpe was *here?*" Kim's twin sister leaned against the kitchen counter and retrieved her margarita. With short spiky red hair, gold hoop earrings and perfect makeup, Kate Cooper looked like a woman confident of her beauty. Her lime-green shirt fit snugly, as did the black Capri pants that hugged her legs. Kate had a gift for fashion and flair, while Kim had a talent for...babies.

"Yep. All six feet of him."

"What'd you do?" She took a swallow of her drink and smiled. "See, isn't it better with extra tequila?"

"I took pictures of his niece, which was why he was here." Kim sipped her drink, then coughed. "Remind me never to let you near my blender again."

"It won't do you any harm." Kate rummaged through the cupboards until she found a bag of tortilla chips, which she poured into one of Kim's yard sale finds. "Where do you *get* this stuff? It's chipped."

"I liked it." She wasn't about to confess to buying it for fifty cents at a yard sale last summer. The blue and white bowl had flaws, but it held the exact amount of popcorn made from a microwave packet. "And it matches the tile."

Kate turned and opened the refrigerator. "Do you still have that pineapple salsa I brought last week?"

"It's in there, behind the milk."

"I see it."

Kim took her drink and the bowl of chips across the room to the small white couch and set everything in the middle of her coffee table, a mahogany relic leftover from their parents' house. She'd painted it white and placed a piece of vintage fabric on top. The blue and pink rose material covered up most of the flaws and blended with the raggedy quilt folded along the back of the couch. The one-bedroom apartment she called home took up the second floor of the house that held their photography business, but it had grown obvious to both women that they needed the space to expand. The business they'd inherited from their father couldn't keep growing unless they had more studio space in which to work.

Once Kate settled herself on the opposite chair, she kicked off her black mules and eyed her sister. "Tell me about him."

"Who?"

"Your doctor."

"He's not my—" she began, but there was no point in disguising the truth. Her sister knew damn well that Stuart Thorpe had, at one time many years ago, been the man of Kim's childish dreams.

"Did he say anything to you?"

"Just that it was good to see me." Kate looked so disappointed that Kim almost laughed.

"He's still one of the best looking men I've ever seen in my life," she admitted.

"Call him. A weekend with a sexy doctor might do you a world of good." Then she stopped, stricken. "I'm sorry," Kate murmured, the smile gone from her face. "I shouldn't tease, especially about this weekend."

"It was a long time ago. And I can deal with

it, honest." She really, really hoped Kate wasn't going to cry.

"Jeff was a real SOB." Now her twin looked as if she was trying to blink back tears.

"Kate—"

"Mom and Dad wanted you to come to Florida this weekend. They wanted to spoil you and show you all the sights."

"I know. Mom's called every night this week hoping I'd change my mind."

"She sent a ticket for you. It's in my purse."

It was silly to feel trapped by one's own family, but Kim felt suffocated by their concern. She didn't want her parents to worry; she dreaded hearing the concern in their voices when they called her to hint about taking a vacation right now.

And all because of Jeff, whom she thought was a good and decent man, had asked her to marry him. Two years ago she'd planned to get married this Memorial Day weekend. They'd set their wedding date, had a celebration dinner with their families gathered together at Jeff's favorite steakhouse, and then four months later he'd confessed he'd thought it over and changed his mind. He was too young to settle down, he'd said. And then he'd run off with his nineteen-year-old office assistant, rumored to be pregnant with his child.

"I'd rather stay home," she said, hoping Kate would understand. Kate usually did, despite their different personalities.

"Not all by yourself?"

"No. With a male stripper who's going to fulfill my every fantasy."

"You wish." But Kate smiled. "But there's always the good doctor. You could call him and tell him you've changed your mind."

"Don't make more of it than it was. It's not as if I ever really went out with him, except for that one blind date. In a group from the apartment house on Wickenden Street, remember? You said he was nice enough."

"It was strictly platonic, though I think he might have kissed me good-night." Kate frowned. "I didn't know you liked him or I wouldn't have gone out with him at all," she said. "Rules are rules."

"It didn't matter." She took another cautious sip of the drink. "He never gave me a second look."

"Because you probably never said one word to him. Even now you could pick up the phone and ask him out to dinner."

"*You* could do that. I can't imagine it." Stuart Thorpe was out of her league. Period.

"I don't know why we're so different."

"We drove Mom crazy." Kate was the demanding one, Kim the quiet one. Kate talked first, but Kim learned to read at age five. Kate talked to strangers while Kim hung back, waiting for her twin to assure her that everything was fine.

"I think we still do." Kate wiggled her painted toenails and stretched her legs. "Are you sure you won't go out with me tonight? There are going to be lots of wonderful men there. Friday night is always good and it will keep your mind off Jeff and that whole mess."

"No, thanks. I'm not brooding or feeling sorry for myself, Kate. Honest."

"Will you call the doctor?"

And say what?

"No. And not in a million years, no matter how much advice you give me."

"Ah, I see. He's the one who got away," Kate said, taking another sip of her drink.

"No." Kim tucked her feet underneath her and remembered her senior year at Rhode Island School of Design, the well-known art school. "He's the one who never came near me at all."

3

SHE WOULDN'T STOP CRYING. No matter what he did, how he held her, what songs he sang or how many bottles he fixed, Brianne would not stop screaming. As far as Stuart was concerned, it was the Friday night from hell.

He prayed Payne wouldn't call and ask how her baby was doing. She'd called twice already, the last time to remind him once again of the photography session.

"Bree, baby, you have to stop," Stuart crooned, a plea that did absolutely no good. He half expected the police to knock on his door and arrest him for violating the local sound ordinance.

"You're hurting Uncle Stuart's ears," he said, holding her against his chest as he patted her back. He'd checked her ears, attempted to look down her throat when she screamed, listened to her heart and caught a glimpse of swollen gums when he'd held her near the reading light by his sofa. Brianne was quite possibly teething, not that he knew anything about babies and teeth.

Not that he knew anything about babies at all.

So he called Brianne's pediatrician and got his answering service, making certain he identified himself as a fellow doctor, and then received a callback from the woman herself.

"Sounds like teething," she said, after asking a few pointed questions. "I usually tell the parents to use baby Tylenol and one of the over-the-counter gum medications made especially for this. And she's not running a fever?"

He didn't think so.

"I'm only the uncle," he tried to explain. "I need help."

He heard her sigh. "Are there any grandmothers nearby who can help you?"

"No." Not bloody likely, he thought, wondering if his mother was still married to husband number four. Or was it five? His father's new lady friend hadn't reached her thirtieth birthday and certainly wasn't the domestic type.

"Well, then, you can always take her into any emergency room, Doctor," she said. "Have her checked out, if you feel the situation warrants it."

The situation warranted a large scotch and a good night's sleep, Stuart figured, but he thanked the woman after she promised he would survive.

Trouble was Stuart didn't dare leave to buy any of that magic stuff, because Temple was supposed to have been here by now. He didn't want her to show up and find him gone. No, his sister could handle this.

"Auntie Temple will be here soon," he chanted, hoping that the sister known as "the wild one" wouldn't stop anywhere on her way from the airport. She should have been in Newport by now; it wouldn't have taken her an hour and a half to get here, even if the traffic was backed up on the bridge.

He grabbed the phone when it rang once. "Temple?"

"Yep, it's me." She also sounded very far away, which was not a good sign. And then she went on to explain that she hadn't been able to leave Mexico, due to an unexpected strike by airport personnel that was rumored to last at least until Monday. "What's the matter, baby brother? You sound desperate."

"I am." He was facing Memorial Day weekend with Bree? "Our niece won't stop crying."

"Maybe you're not holding her the right way."

"I'm holding her the right way," he insisted. "I called her doctor. She's teething."

"You haven't called Payne, have you?"

"You're kidding, right?"

"She's going to kill me for this." Now Temple was catching on, Stuart thought. "Don't tell her I'm in Mexico."

"She'll find out. You know she'll call."

"Don't answer the phone. I know," she said, sounding brighter. "Drive Bree around in the car. That's what Payne does when nothing else works."

"Drive around when she's screaming at the top of her lungs? How does that make sense?"

"Just try it. I don't suppose you date any divorced mothers?"

"Not if I can help it." He didn't tell her he'd called a couple of his female friends for help, but neither had seemed very interested in discussing infant care.

"Then you're screwed."

"And it's your fault."

"Look, I'm not going to pretend it's any kind

of hardship being stuck in Puerto Vallarta with a gorgeous fireman named Hank who's built like a Greek god and says he hasn't been with a woman in—well, never mind. He's a little rough around the edges, but that's the way I like—"

He closed his eyes. "Please, Temple. For God's sake, no details."

"Right." She chuckled. "When did you suddenly turn prudish?"

"Temple, I'm begging you. Get on a plane. Any plane. Come home. Can't you hear your niece screaming for you?" He held the receiver close to Bree's open mouth and let Temple get a blast of the baby's anger.

"Sorry, pal. Circumstances beyond my control and all that. Besides, laying on the guilt doesn't work with me," was all she said before she hung up.

Brianne looked at him and screamed even louder, if that was possible.

"How do you feel about cars? Drugstores? Tylenol?" he asked, holding her to his shoulder. "What kind of music do you want to listen to? Jazz? Blues? Classical? Or classic rock?"

She continued to scream into her uncle's ear.

And then she messed her pants.

"HELP," WAS ALL STUART said, standing there on her back doorstep with a sobbing baby on his shoulder. Kim didn't know why she held out her arms, but he looked relieved and handed Brianne to her. The poor little girl was heated and damp, her face wet with tears as she nestled against Kim's chest.

"What have you done to her?"

"I think," he said. "It's the other way around."

"Is there something wrong with her?" Kim stepped aside and let him into the back foyer of the studio. It was true that he didn't look any better than he had three hours ago. He wore the same stained rumpled clothes and he looked close to exhaustion. But still, of course, tremendously handsome. The "movie star" face and the killer smile were a lethal combination, even when Stuart was grubby and tired.

"She's teething," he said, hoarse. "I talked to her pediatrician, who explained it to me."

Brianne hiccupped and then let out another wail. Kim forgot to ask why he was here or how he'd discovered she lived above the studio or any other questions her more clever twin would have uttered. She snuggled the baby against her and led Stuart upstairs. "Poor baby," she murmured. "She misses her mommy, I'll bet."

"Yeah," Stuart said behind her. "So do I."

"What happened to her aunt? Didn't you say—"

"Airplane strike. She's stuck in Mexico with a fireman—never mind," he said, joining her on the top landing. He followed her through the open door of her apartment. "Trying to explain Temple right now would take too much energy."

"But what are you doing *here?*" Surely he didn't think she knew anything about teething.

"I couldn't think of anywhere else to go. She liked you this afternoon," he said. "She stopped crying when you held her."

"That's different." Kim sat down in the black-painted rocking chair that had belonged to her grandmother and felt the child stiffen in her arms. Once she began to rock, though, Brianne once again relaxed against her. "That was professional."

"I gave her Tylenol," Stuart continued, as if he hadn't heard her. He sat in the middle of the couch and leaned back. "I rubbed her gums with medicine that's supposed to numb the pain. I changed her diapers a dozen times."

"But you're a doctor," Kim pointed out, still amazed this particular man had ended up in her living room. "You don't know what to do?"

"I'm a vascular surgeon," he said. "I haven't done anything with pediatrics since I was in med school."

"Did you call her mother?"

"Payne?" He grimaced. "I couldn't. She's got enough to handle right now, with her husband away and her in-laws needing her. I don't think her mother-in-law's prognosis is very good."

"I'm sorry."

"Yeah. Me, too. I don't dare give Payne anything else to worry about right now." His gaze dropped to Brianne. "Thank God she's stopped crying."

"The poor thing." Kim was glad Kate had left a little while ago. While her sister would urge her to go out on a date, she would be suspicious of a man who appeared needing help with a baby. *Sucker*, Kate would say, shaking her head. *You let everyone take advantage of you.*

At this moment, with the warmth of a baby snuggled against her, Kim didn't care.

"So I took a chance you were still here," Stuart said. "I got the impression you lived upstairs from the way you and your neighbors talked."

"And she really isn't your daughter?"

"I swear," he said, holding up his right hand. "I'm Uncle Stuart, that's all."

"I'm not any kind of a baby expert," she said, rubbing the child's back.

"You're doing better than I was."

"Isn't this a little strange?"

"Not really. Payne thought Temple would take over until Monday. Temple's a little wild, but she's good with Brianne and she has a degree in—"

"I mean strange that you're here," she explained. "We don't really know each other."

"Did I go out with you once?"

"You don't remember?"

"Not really. I was a resident then and I don't remember much about those years except that I was always tired."

"So what are you going to do now?"

"I hadn't thought past this," he said, closing his eyes as he rested his head against the back of the couch.

"This?"

"Silence. No screaming, sobbing or wailing."

"Take your niece home and put her to bed. She must be exhausted enough to sleep."

"Easy for you to say." He opened his eyes and gazed around the room. "Do you *live* here?"

"Yes." She tried to see the place through his eyes. It was a little crowded. More than a little, she supposed, but she was used to it. She loved to use antique props in her photographs and there wasn't much room downstairs. Vintage hats hung on the walls, an armoire held soft linen children's dresses of various sizes, an old bicycle sat in the corner by the television and an assortment of baskets, wicker chairs, baby furniture and vintage toys lined the edges of the room, leaving the center of the living area open for the sofa, coffee table and rocking chair. "I think it's cozy."

"It is." He yawned. So did Brianne. "If I begged, would you come home with me? To baby-sit, I mean."

She knew what he meant. She'd never exactly inspired lust in men who looked like Stuart. Even Robbie was less interested in her body than he was in her ability to photograph *his*.

"You could call an agency," she suggested. "Maybe they have emergency nannies."

"Payne won't let strangers near her child."

She didn't point out that she was a stranger and so far Brianne hadn't complained. "Do you have any other family who could help you?" What she really wanted to know was why he hadn't called one of his many girlfriends to lend a hand. Surely there would be at least one who would leap at the opportunity to show what a good Mrs. Thorpe she could be.

"Aside from my sister, there is no one remotely maternal in my family." He closed his eyes again. "If you won't come home with us, would you let me rest here a minute?"

"Sure." She didn't know what else to say anyway, so sitting in silence didn't bother her. If gorgeous Stuart Thorpe wanted to take a nap on her sofa while his niece slept on her chest, well, she would enjoy it for as long as it lasted. She rocked gently and tried to visualize a conversation with her sister. *Kate*, she would say. *Guess who showed up at my door last night. Stuart Thorpe. No, I'm not kidding. He was here, larger than life. Why? Because he needed a baby-sitter, that's why.*

She wouldn't hurt Kate's feelings by explaining that this was much better than one of those blind dates her twin was always trying to fix her up with. She never knew what to say or how to flirt. More than one drink made her sick, she couldn't swallow sushi and wasn't coordinated enough to dance the two-step or engage in exciting and original sexual positions, not that her dates ever got that far.

No, she was happy rocking. And when Stuart started to snore, she didn't even mind.

It was nice not to be alone.

"ANNA." PATRICK DIDN'T waste time with a lot of extra words when he used the telephone.

"What?" He could hear the television in the background.

"He's over at her house." Patrick could stand at his telephone mounted on the kitchen wall and look through to the living room window that faced the photography studio.

"Who?"

"The doctor with the baby." There was no mistaking that fancy car, parked right there in the driveway next to the house. "Kimmy's lights are on upstairs."

"Just a minute," Anna grumbled. "I can't hear a thing." She must have found her remote control because the television noise stopped. "Now, what's going on?"

"You heard me," he said. "That fancy doctor is back to see Kimmy and I'll bet this time he's up to no good."

"How do you know that?"

"I may be old, but I'm not stupid. That fella is up to something. Look out your window."

"Maybe he likes Kim. Maybe they're having supper together."

"It's too late for supper. She didn't come over for your sausage and peppers, did she?"

"No, but I saved some for her," Anna said. "For tomorrow. You know I always make too much."

"I know." The fact that Anna always made "too much" was one of the major highlights of his life. His wife—bless her sweet soul—had never made lasagna, Italian meatballs, minestrone or stuffed eggplant. Anna's homemade spaghetti sauce, fried dough and frosted anise cookies gave a man something to live for.

"You worry too much," she told him. "Because you don't like his car."

"He's too good-looking," Pat insisted. "Too smooth. Not Kimmy's type at all."

"Look." He heard Anna sigh. "She was supposed to get married this weekend. Tomorrow, even. So he's keeping her company. What's the matter with that? She can't live like a nun be-cause her boyfriend ran off with another woman."

He didn't know why not. At least Kim wouldn't get her heart broken again. "Well, I don't like it."

"Tomorrow we'll all go to the yard sales to-gether," she said. "Kim likes that and we'll keep her busy. Then Kate's got something set up for that night, so she won't be alone."

"She's not alone now," he felt the need to point out. "What if he's some kind of serial killer?"

"I looked him up in the phone book. He's a real doctor with a fancy office in Providence up by Rhode Island Hospital. And Kim used to know him, remember? If he was a serial killer he'd be in jail by now."

"There's a new serial killer born every day."

"Go to bed," Anna said. "Or go watch TV. *Antiques Roadshow* is gonna be on in a minute."

"All right." He had no intention of watching television. "What time are we leaving tomor-row?"

"Come over before seven," she said. "I made a list and you can check the directions. And quit your worrying."

He hung up without agreeing to anything and returned to the front window. Quit worrying? Go to bed? When Kim—innocent, sweet Kim—was the target of an oversexed fancy doctor's lust?

No way in hell.

4

THE PHONE WOKE HIM. Stuart didn't know where he was, but as a surgeon he was accustomed to waking quickly, accustomed to taking advantage of a quick nap whenever he could. So he managed to pull the cell phone from his belt and push the right button to answer even before he realized his location.

"Yeah?"

"Where on *earth* have you been?" Payne did not sound pleased.

Stuart blinked and Kim Cooper's strange apartment came into focus. There was one lamp lit and the room was empty. No baby. No Kim. He was in deep shit.

"Payne," he said, not answering the question. "How's everything?"

"Better." She sighed. "How's Bree? Is she okay? Did she smile for the photographer?"

"She's teething," he said, hoping that would bring his sister back to Rhode Island immediately. "I called her doctor to find out what to do."

"Good. Tylenol and Orajel?"

"Yeah. She hasn't cried for a while now." Stuart got to his feet and crossed the apartment.

"Why aren't you answering your phone? I went crazy until I remembered you finally bought a cell phone and then I had to call your service to get the number."

"It's just for emergencies," he said, peering down a narrow hall. He hoped that Kim and his niece were around somewhere. "I tend to forget I have it."

"Are you at Temple's? She's not answering her phone either."

"Temple is…delayed," he said, bracing himself for the onslaught, but there was silence. "Payne? Did you hear me?"

"Delayed? What does that mean?"

"There's an airplane strike in Mexico."

"There's a *man* in Mexico is more like it. What did she say?"

"Well—"

"Never mind. You'll have to bring Bree to me, then."

At first taking the baby to Payne sounded like a good idea. And then Stuart remembered how

loud his niece could scream. Five or six hours—
maybe more—in a car with a teething baby
didn't sound like a good plan. Then again,
spending the entire weekend caring for a teething baby didn't sound like a piece of cake either.

"Stuart? Are you there?"

He peeked around the corner and saw Kim
sitting on her bed, a book opened on her lap, the
baby asleep beside her. The light was low, the
bed wide and he had the strangest urge to join
them, to deposit Bree into a more appropriate
bed and then convince the pretty photographer
to join him under the covers.

But Kim looked up and put her finger to her
lips, so Stuart got the message. *Don't you dare
wake her.*

"I'm here," he whispered, backing out of the
room. "I don't want to wake Bree."

Payne began to give him directions to Rockland, Maine, while he assured her he could find
his way north and yes, he had the phone numbers she'd left him and no, he wouldn't drive
over the speed limit.

"I'm thirty-five years old," he reminded his
sister. "A respected member of the medical
community."

"But you're not a father."

"I can still drive north. I can read a compass. I can follow a map."

"Maybe I should come home," was his sister's reply. "Maybe—"

"No." Now it was a matter of male pride. "We'll be there tomorrow. What is it, about six hours from here?"

"About, depending on traffic. It's a holiday weekend."

"Fine."

"How is she? Do you think she misses me?" Now Payne sounded teary.

"Of course she does," he said, using his soothing doctor voice. "And she'll be fine. We can both survive overnight."

"Promise?"

"Of course." Because Kim Cooper was taking care of the baby.

After a few more words to console his sister, Stuart turned off the phone and returned to the doorway of Kim's bedroom.

She wasn't his type, he reminded himself. A pair of lovely, slender legs stretched across a shabby quilt, though. And her bare feet were crossed at the ankles and would tempt a lesser man to rub her toes and then higher, uncrossing her legs and laying himself on top an appealing, satin-skinned female.

The woman looked up at him, a question in her eyes that had nothing to do with sex.

"My sister," he whispered, stepping into the small room. "Bree's mother. She wants me to bring her to Maine."

"Right now?" Her own whisper was strangely intimate and put his senses on high alert. There was nothing more enjoyable than the sight of a pretty woman in bed, and this one was no exception.

"Tomorrow." He looked around for someplace to sit, but the room only held a dresser with a television perched on top, a trunk topped with neatly folded quilts and a rickety-looking child's chair. Kim solved the problem by moving her legs so he had room to sit on the edge of the bed.

Bree didn't stir. She lay on her back, a pacifier tucked into her mouth and her breathing was deep and regular.

"How did you get her to sleep?"

"I rocked her," Kim explained, setting a hardcover book on the nightstand.

"That's amazing." He should have thought

of that, not that he had a rocking chair. But he could have bought one easily enough.

"Not really. I think her medicine kicked in. And I imagine she's had a long day."

"So has Uncle Stuart." He watched as Kim made an attempt to smooth her shirt, then self-consciously pushed her tousled hair away from her face. So she wasn't used to having men in her bedroom. He'd bet a month's income that there would be no men's shaving equipment in the bathroom, no condoms tucked in the night-stand drawer, no extra toothbrushes or cans of shaving cream.

"I guess you're not used to babies."

"No. I should be sorry we barged in on you," he said. "But I'm not. Bree and I both needed the rest. Did I snore?"

"Yes."

He winced. "Sorry."

"I'm sure you've been told that before."

"No comment."

"Okay." She laughed softly. He was surprised again at how pretty she was, in a wholesome kind of way. Maybe there *was* a man—or men—in her life.

"Do you like lobster?"

"Yes. Why?"

"We could have dinner tomorrow night," he said, deciding he was the smartest man on the planet. "In Rockland, Maine."

"That's where your sister is," she said, giving him a look that was not exactly enthusiastic.

"It's on Penobscot Bay. It's supposed to be very picturesque." Damn. Now he sounded like a travel agent.

"I can't help you out tomorrow," Kim said. "Sorry."

"It was just a thought." Well, he probably deserved that. He wasn't exactly his most attractive self, not in wrinkled, food-stained clothes and having snored on her couch. "No big deal."

"I'm sure you can find someone else."

"Someone else?" He looked at his sleeping niece, deceptively sweet-looking with her eyes shut and her mouth around a pacifier. She'd spit it out whenever he'd tried to give it to her, the little rascal. She was almost as ornery as her mother.

"To help you with Bree."

"I doubt it." He met her gaze and hoped he looked pathetic enough that she would feel sorry for him and relent. But she looked away and slid off the bed.

"I hate to see you wake her up," she said, looking down at the sleeping child.

"She's going to scream," he promised. "Your neighbor will have to fix his hearing aid again." Kim frowned, meaning Stuart knew he had a chance to actually get a few hours sleep if he was shameless enough to take it. "Could we stay here until she wakes up?"

She turned to look at him, so he did his best to look pathetic.

"She'll want another bottle in a couple of hours," he said. "And then we'll leave."

"It's after ten," she pointed out. "She doesn't sleep through the night?"

"Not yet," he assured her. He didn't have a clue how long his niece slept, but he was willing to assume Bree would get hungry again before dawn.

"We'll have to put pillows around her so she can't fall off the bed."

"I'll do anything you want," he heard himself say.

"You'd better take the bed—and the baby— so you'll be the one she wakes up. I'll sleep on the couch."

"Are you sure?" He didn't think forcing Kim out of her own bed was a good idea.

"Just try not to snore and wake her up."

He couldn't help smiling. She looked so serious. "I'll do my best," he promised.

"THERE'S ONE BORN EVERY minute," Kate declared, standing in the door to Kim's bedroom. "And I get to see this with my own eyes."

"It's not the way it looks," Kim said, urging her out of the way so she could leave the room. "And keep your voice down."

"You have a man and a baby in your bed at six o'clock on a Saturday morning and you expect me to be quiet?" Her twin laughed, but she put her hand over her mouth before any sound could escape.

"Shh." Kim hurried down the hall and hoped the coffee was ready. She'd taken a quick shower and dressed in shorts and a T-shirt, but she still hadn't decided how to spend the day. Her sister's surprising arrival at this hour of the morning meant Kate had her own ideas what Kim should do, and Kim knew it would be difficult to head off her twin. "I need caffeine."

"You need more than caffeine," Kate muttered, following her down the hall. "When I left last night you were going to make yourself a toasted cheese sandwich and go to bed early instead of going out with me. How did your night get so exciting?"

"It wasn't that exciting," she said, though it certainly had been more entertaining than watching television. She filled two mugs with coffee and handed one to her sister.

"Tell me everything." Kate took her coffee over to the small glass-topped patio table Kim used for dining and sat down in one of two iron chairs. "Why is Stuart Thorpe in your bed?"

"I thought about you last night," Kim mused. "I imagined having this conversation."

"And?"

"He needed help with the baby and I was the only one he could think of."

"He used you as a baby-sitter?" Kate's expression was one of horror.

"It gets worse." She took another sip of her coffee and remembered that today was to have been her wedding day. She glanced out the window and saw that it was going to be sunny.

"Yeah," Kate said. "He slept in your bed."

"I wasn't in there with him." She didn't add that he was going to leave when the baby woke up, but Bree had slept through the night. She also didn't explain that she had given Stuart the bed so he could be near his niece.

Her twin gave her worried look. "You're in over your head, Kim."

"He appeared at my door asking for help. What was I supposed to do?"

"You didn't have to give him your bed." Kate stood up and peered over to the other side of the room. "You slept on the couch?"

"His sister got stuck in Mexico."

"Like that makes any kind of sense." Kate sat down again and took a sip of coffee. "We're going out tonight. I've fixed you up with an accountant from East Providence whose hobby is refinishing furniture."

"I really don't—"

"He's thirty, attractive and steady as a rock," her sister continued. "We're going out to dinner and then maybe to that new comedy club for drinks."

"Kate—"

"You can't be alone today. Or tonight. I promised Mom I'd keep you busy."

"I don't want to be kept busy. I have plenty of work to do here and besides, I'm not brooding over my wedding." The more she thought about it, the more she realized she'd been lucky to escape a lifetime of Jeff's infidelities. "You know, I'll bet anything Jeff's already cheating on his wife."

Kate leaned forward. "You're very vulnerable right now. You have every right to be bitter."

"I'm not bitter, just realistic. Jeff was a very good liar, don't you think? Don't answer that," she added quickly. "I don't want to talk about him. What are you doing here so early?"

"I told you, I promised Mom." She turned toward the door at the same time Kim did. "Uh-oh. You have company."

Kim heard knocking downstairs and could guess who it was. "It's Pat and Anna."

"Oh, good." Kate set her coffee cup down and stood. "I'll go let them in."

"You can't." Kim hopped up to stop her. "They'll wake up the baby."

"I'll tell them to be quiet. Are you going to yard sales today?"

"They'd asked, but—"

"Good. I'll meet you for breakfast later and then we'll go shopping for some great outfits for tonight. Providence Place or Warwick Mall?" Kate crossed the room and bounded down the stairs to the back door. Kim heard

Patrick and Anna's voices as her sister let them inside.

Kim didn't want to go shopping. The phrase "great outfits" filled her with dread, since Kate's version would be something revealing, sexy and uncomfortably tight.

"Oh, boy," Anna said, stepping inside the apartment. "I'm not used to stairs so much anymore."

"I was going to come over if I decided to go with you," Kim reminded her. "I'm still not sure—"

"Oh, I need the exercise," Anna said, cutting off her words.

Patrick was right behind her, but the old man didn't look the least concerned with the stairs. "There's a strange car in your parking lot, Kim. Did you know that?"

"Uh, yes. It's fine. I know who it belongs to." She went over to the cupboard and took out two more mugs. Keeping her voice down, she asked, "Does anyone want coffee?"

"I told them to whisper," Kate said. "But I didn't say why."

Anna held up the newspaper. "Do you want to see our list? There's some good ones over by Roger Williams Park we'll go to first."

Patrick looked down the hall and then toward Kim. "No coffee for me, Kimmy. And why are we whispering?"

"The baby's asleep." She crossed her arms in front of her chest and felt like she was on trial. Anna's mouth fell open and Pat shook his head.

"What baby?"

"Brianne, from yesterday."

"I knew that fella was up to no good," he muttered. "I knew it the minute I saw him."

"Oh, never mind the doctor," Kate said, retrieving her coffee cup from the table. "I've got Kim fixed up with a perfectly suitable guy tonight. And we're going shopping—after the yard sales, of course."

"You're coming with us, Kate?" Anna looked thrilled. "The more the merrier, that's what I say. Did you bring plenty of change?"

"Uh, I might get some work done here while you're out finding—"

"Good morning." Stuart came down the hall with Bree against his chest. The baby looked sleepy, but she didn't cry when she saw four unfamiliar people staring at her and her uncle.

"Good morning," Kim heard herself say as if nothing whatsoever was unusual about a man walking out of her bedroom on a Saturday morning. "Would you like some coffee?"

"Sure." He walked barefoot into the kitchen. Even though he'd slept in his clothes, his dark hair was rumpled and he sported a day's growth of dark whiskers, he was still as good-looking as ever. Brianne's dark hair and eyes matched his own, so the resemblance between them was striking. "Thanks."

He looked at the others. "Everyone's up early this morning. Hi, Kate."

"Hello. It's been a long time. Cute baby you have there." Even Kate looked a little stunned. Anna was the only one who didn't seem to notice that anything was out of the ordinary.

"There's that little sweetheart," she said. "Are you a sleepy girl this morning?"

The baby smiled but stayed snuggled against her uncle's neck. No man should look that good this early in the morning, Kim decided as Stuart approached her to take his coffee.

"Do you take anything in it?"

"Just black," he said, setting the mug on the counter out of Bree's way.

"We should get going," Patrick said, but he looked at Stuart as if he wondered if it was safe to leave the man alone in the apartment.

"I'll go, too," Kate said. "I'll take you all out to breakfast afterward, and then Kim and I are hitting the malls."

"Good for you," Anna said, while Patrick suggested to Stuart that he should be at the hospital checking on patients, shouldn't he?

Kim didn't want to shop for shoes and clothes, and though she loved her neighbors, she really didn't want to spend the morning looking for bargains, either. They were all trying to keep her mind off her broken heart and no one wanted to hear that her heart wasn't broken. Her pride, maybe, had been injured. Not because of Jeff—that was old news—but because everyone had such pity for her.

It was embarrassing.

"I'm not going today," she said, interrupting the conversations swirling around her. Even Bree, gripping her uncle's ear, had begun to babble. Of course no one paid the least bit of attention to her, now that Kate had launched into a detailed description of tonight's date.

"I'm not going today," Kim announced once again, this time raising her voice to compete with the others.

"What?" Kate turned to look at her.

"Why not?" Patrick turned to Stuart as if it was all his fault that she was acting strangely.

"Stuart's invited me to Maine for the weekend," she said, avoiding her sister's gaze. "We're leaving this morning."

5

"DON'T SAY A WORD."

"Nothing?" Stuart completed the complicated arrangement of putting Brianne in her car seat and shut the back door. He walked around to the driver's side of the car and slid behind the wheel. "Are you sure? I have a lot of questions that have been building up since you suddenly announced you were taking me up on my travel invitation."

"Save your questions for later. I'll let you know when."

And here he'd thought she was shy.

"You feel sorry for me."

"No."

"For Brianne?"

"Not really."

"I didn't think so." He glanced toward her for a look at those legs again. She'd crossed them, and a leather sandal dangling from one bare foot. "You know, you should always wear shorts. Or skirts. Very short skirts."

She ignored him. And then she reached into her purse and pulled out a pair of sunglasses, which didn't intimidate him in the least. She could hide those green eyes and turn her face toward the window, but that didn't change the fact that she was going to Maine with him.

It was his lucky day. Brianne had slept through the night and would be turned over to the loving arms of her mother this afternoon; after today he would have the remaining two days of a four-day weekend to enjoy. The sun was shining, the sky was blue and now he had help with the baby.

"So I guess you thought about that lobster dinner," he said, backing out the driveway and onto the empty street. She ignored him, but he noticed she waved goodbye to her sister, whose face was identical to Kim's. It was a little eerie, but no one could mistake the two women. Kate was high energy and Kim was peace and quiet. "Or was it my charm that you couldn't resist?"

"You said you needed a baby-sitter. Could we leave it at that?"

"You're not a morning person, I see." Stuart guided the car onto the main street and headed north, toward the 95 on-ramp. "I have to stop at my place first and get some clean clothes.

You've probably noticed that I look like an escaped convict."

She smiled, which encouraged him.

"If you'd watch Bree for ten minutes, I could even take a shower," he bargained.

"That's what I'm here for."

"I doubt it," he muttered, knowing there was more to this than Kim suddenly deciding to help out an old acquaintance. "What are you running away from? Yard sales? Blind dates? Shopping? I thought women liked all those things."

"I do. Sometimes." Kim turned to look at him again when he stopped for a red light. "It was just a little...suffocating, that's all."

He couldn't see her eyes—those damn glasses covered them—but he thought he saw her lower lip quiver. Oh, hell. He hoped she wasn't going to cry. There had to be a man involved. What kind of man would make Kim Cooper cry? He had to be a real prick, that was certain. "Ah, you've dumped a boyfriend and he's stalking you."

"You have a very vivid imagination," she said. "Do you watch a lot of television?"

"Female mud wrestling is a personal favorite," he said, hoping to make her laugh. It didn't work, so after a few minutes of silence Stuart tried again. "I thought your friend Patrick was going to take a punch at me."

"He's a little protective," she admitted. "I didn't mean to upset anyone, but—"

He waited for an explanation.

"But?" he urged.

"I decided that even being a baby-sitter was better than going out on a blind date."

Stuart wasn't sure how this baby-sitting thing had gotten blown out of proportion. "You're not exactly in junior high, working for four bucks an hour. You're doing a friend a favor. During a family emergency, no less."

"I sound so noble."

"Yes. Very self-sacrificing," he agreed, grinning at her. She ignored him again and returned to looking out the window. There was little traffic on the interstate this early in the morning, despite the fact that it was a holiday weekend. He'd be at his place before eight and they could be on the road north by eight-thirty.

"Where are we going?" She sounded wary, as if she was being kidnapped.

"Rockland. It's on the coast—"

"I mean where are we going *now?*"

"Oh. Newport. For clean clothes and baby food."

"That's where you live?"

"Yes. Why are you so surprised?"

"I thought—never mind."

"Where did you think I lived?"

"Providence. Or Cranston. You said you were driving the baby around last night so I didn't think you lived forty-five minutes away."

"I drove her around a lot." He glanced in the rearview mirror to see his niece sound asleep in her seat. "She likes the car."

"I don't know why I'm doing this," Kim said, almost as if she was talking to herself. She turned and looked at the baby. "You're not going to have any trouble. She'll probably sleep all the way to Maine."

Stuart disagreed. "I couldn't get that lucky. Any minute now she's going to wake up and yell at me about something. She takes after Payne."

"You only have the two sisters?"

"Thank God." Stuart glanced in the mirror again and satisfied himself that Brianne wasn't going to scream at him anytime soon. Maybe they would make it all the way home before she woke up.

"That's not very nice."

"They're both older than me and they won't quit bossing me around. I'm the youngest."

"The youngest." She sighed. "I see. That explains a lot."

He thought maybe he liked it better when Kim didn't want to talk.

PATRICK DIDN'T THINK Kate was often speechless, but Kimmy's sudden departure stunned even the "fancy twin," as he thought of her. He'd helped Anna down the stairs, but by the time they'd reached the yard Kim, the baby and her fancy doctor were already driving down the street. He sure hoped that young fellow wasn't the type to speed, because that car looked like it could go fast.

"We're gonna be late for the big one on Pontiac Avenue," Anna said, looking at the list she still held in her hand.

"Anna, aren't you worried? Kim just went off with that man. It's just not right, that's what I say." He looked over to Kate. "What do you think about all of this, missy? You got anything to say?"

"Nope." But she didn't look too happy. "I guess she didn't want to go to the malls."

"You still want to come with us to the yard sales, Kate? We've got plenty of room in the front seat," Anna said. "We always have a pretty good time and you might even find something for that fancy apartment of yours. Then we can go out to breakfast, if you want."

"Thanks, Mrs. G., but I think I'll get some work done in the darkroom this morning. Maybe next time." She looked down the street, but of course the Mercedes had disappeared. Anna reached out and patted Kate's arm.

"I don't know what you're so worried about, honey. That doctor is a nice young man," Anna insisted, urging them to the sidewalk where Patrick had parked his truck. "And he's very handsome, too. Maybe he's just what she needs right now."

Kate opened her mouth as if she was going to say something, but then she must have changed her mind, because Patrick noticed she clamped her lips together before she turned and went back into the house.

"Kim doesn't need a man like that," Patrick grumbled, pulling his keys out of his pants pocket. "He'll just take advantage of her good nature, that's all."

Anna gave him a gentle shove and laughed. "And she might enjoy herself, too, you old grump. Have you forgotten what it's like to be young?"

"Yes. No." He caught Anna's eye and couldn't help smiling a little. "I just don't want her to get hurt."

She shrugged. "Hey, we all get hurt. We all survive. That's life."

Patrick thought it might be a little early for Italian philosophy, but he kept his mouth shut and helped his friend into the truck.

SHE HAD TO BE OUT OF her mind. As Stuart parked the car beside a white three-story mansion on Bellevue Avenue, Kim Cooper decided that at some point in the last eighteen—oh, dear, was that all it was?—hours she had somehow lost control of her life. And she liked her life, her family, her work. She loved her life, her family, and her work. The only dark spot was the loss of the lilac garden and she still had hope that Providence Photography could buy the property. And if she was lonely once in a while and longed for a family—okay, and babies—of her own to photograph, she told herself that she was still quite young.

At twenty-six, she had no reason to hear the tick of her biological clock. She certainly had no reason to be worried about her future. When the car stopped, Kim realized they were parked near one of the most beautiful homes she'd ever seen.

"…turned into condos," Stuart said. "A lot of the big old houses around here have been converted into condominiums or apartments."

It had four massive white pillars flanking the front door. A driveway curved around the entrance and then back out to Bellevue Avenue, the wealthiest street in Rhode Island, if not in all of New England. They'd passed larger mansions, the kind that gave tours and hosted grand fund-raising events. Kim herself had paid admission to several of them and enjoyed every minute of imagining what "The Gilded Age" had been like for the Vanderbilts and Astors and their friends. And now here she was in front of a smaller version of one of those grand houses.

"It's beautiful," she managed to say.

"Thanks. I was lucky to get it before the real estate boom."

Kim stepped out of the car onto the gravel parking area and then reached back inside the car for her bag. Stuart managed to get Bree out of her car seat, but the baby wasn't happy about being moved.

"Uh-oh," he said. "I think she knows where she is and she doesn't like it."

Sure enough, Bree's face crunched into an expression of absolute fury and she let out a shriek that made a group of sparrows explode from an enormous beech tree. Stuart grimaced and handed her to Kim, who carefully took the baby into her arms.

"Gee, thanks."

"Don't mention it." He reached back into the car and retrieved the diaper bag and a bundle of pink blankets. "Work your magic."

Bree continued to scream her protest at being removed from the car. "Did I tell you that I don't really know anything about babies?"

"What?"

Kim raised her voice so he could hear her over the shrieking. "I don't know anything about babies!"

He shrugged. "Hey, you know more than I do. Come on, ladies. It's time for the man of the house to clean himself up."

Man of the house? Man of the mansion was more appropriate. She followed him across the gravel area to the massive double front doors, which he unlocked and opened. He ushered her into a wide hall, with a high ceiling from which two glass chandeliers hung. Straight ahead was a multiwindowed wall with glass doors that led to a sloping grassy lawn. To the right was a curving staircase, which Stuart bypassed. He led her to a door on the left, at the far end of the hall.

"Come on in." He pushed the door open and let her and Bree step inside. It was a huge living room, with marble floors and white walls and black leather furniture. Clean, too, as one would expect from a doctor, she noticed. Especially the kind of doctor who could afford a cleaning lady.

"I think this was originally a music room," he said, pointing to a white marble fireplace adorned with carvings of harps. A bank of windows faced the back lawn and let in light. "There's a small kitchen area tucked behind that wall, then my bedroom and bathroom over there." He pointed to the far end of the room where an oversized door was propped open with a piece of driftwood.

"It's enormous," was all she could think to say.

"Most of the condos have about two rooms, but they're big," he said, lifting Bree out of Kim's arms. He walked over to a playpen set up by the windows and plopped her inside of it so that she was on her back. "Here, sweetheart. Give Kim a rest and look at the birds."

"I don't mind holding her," she said, wondering if the other residents of the house tolerated the sound of a crying child. Bree surprised her by appearing content.

"Give me ten minutes, all right?" Stuart ran his fingers through his hair as he stood close to her. "Make yourself comfortable. Make some coffee, help yourself to anything in the fridge, and I'll be as fast as I can."

"Take your time," she told him, wishing she hadn't left her camera in the car. Kate would love to see this place.

He hesitated, then leaned down and gave her a quick kiss.

"Thanks," he said, oblivious to her surprise at having those warm lips touch hers. "I won't forget this."

Kim didn't think this adventure would disappear from her memory bank any time soon either, but she kept silent. It was a puny little friendship kiss, nothing to be pleased about. She watched him stride toward his bedroom, but before he disappeared she called out, "How long is it to Rockland?"

"About five or six hours, I think," he said, turning to grin at her. "I'm not really sure. We'll have to get a map."

"Good idea," she said, and then he was gone, the door shut behind him. She needed more than a map. Kim Cooper was well aware that she needed to keep her mind off Stuart Thorpe's lips and her brain focused on self-preservation, even if her body had somehow gotten the idea that kissing was good and sex would be even better.

Women like her did not end up taking showers with men like Stuart, she told herself. She might fantasize a little, and she might blush at the ideas in her head, but in the end she would check on the baby, find the kitchen and make coffee.

Because she didn't really want anything from this man except a reason to get out of town.

"I can't believe it's this complicated." Stuart eyed the array of baby furniture and paraphernalia in his living room and wondered how he would fit it all in his car.

"Well, you probably should bring all these things in case your sister needs them. And we have to take enough bottles and food for the day, plus extra, which is why I fixed the cooler."

Ah, the cooler. He'd left it on the counter, ready for a picnic on the beach with a luscious bartender from that place on Thames Street. Now it held ice cubes, baby bottles and two cans of cola. He reached in and replaced one of the colas with a bottle of Sam Adams.

"For later," he said, when Kim gave him a questioning look. "Do you want one, too?"

"Please."

He removed the other cola can and shoved another beer into the ice cubes. "You watch Bree and I'll load the car," he said, setting the lid on the cooler. "You're sure we need to take all this stuff?"

"You can call your sister and ask." Kim smiled at him, which made Stuart realize that her eyes were a very unusual shade of green. Maybe it was the light.

"No way. She's left three messages on my voice mail already this morning." After listening to the second set of detailed driving directions, he'd decided against checking his messages for the rest of the day.

"Did you tell her Bree was okay?"

He grinned. "Yeah. I left a message on *her* voice mail." Stuart picked up his car keys, the cooler and the folded high chair and went through the front door that Kim held open for him. It took longer than he imagined it would to load up the car, especially since the playpen ended up wedged in front of the back seat, but they managed to fit everything in.

"I'll bet your Mercedes has never looked so domestic," she said, laughing up at him as she held Bree against her hip. "Your socialite girlfriends should see you now."

He took the baby from her and tried to ignore the feeling of her skin against his fingertips when he brushed her arms. "Socialite girlfriends?"

"I read the newspaper." Kim bent to pick up Bree's sock from the driveway.

"Yeah, well, I end up going to a lot of fundraisers." Which was an understatement. Lately he'd grown tired of the latest round of charity events and had even vowed to retire his tuxedo and take up something more exciting, like bowling. He took the sock and tossed it on the back seat, on top of a pile of blankets.

"You're very photogenic."

He figured she was teasing and ignored the comment. He managed to get Bree into her car seat without too much trouble. "You know, I might be getting good at this. She didn't yell at me this time."

"Do we know where we're going?"

"Yep." He held open the door for her with a dramatic flourish, hoping she'd smile at him again. "I'll get a map when we stop for gas."

"Good."

"We don't *need* a map," he said, admiring those legs of hers again. He could easily circle her ankle with his hand. "I can get to Boston and then pick up 95, which takes us almost the rest of the way."

"I'd feel better if I could see for myself," she said, so he closed her door.

Yeah, well, he'd feel better if he'd spent his weekend sleeping late and getting laid, not necessarily in that order. And yet here he was feeling guilty over one measly kiss, not even a kiss, really. More like a "thank you" with lips. Lips that stayed closed.

There would be no more kissing, he told himself. Otherwise she might get out at the first town and call her sister to pick her up and then where would he be? Alone in a car with a teething baby. And neither he nor Brianne had much patience with each other. Bree wanted her mommy and Stuart wanted...well, never mind what he wanted. He got in his car and tried not to look at the length of silken female thigh so close to him. If he reached out he could slide his fingertips along that warm skin and see what she felt like.

"What's the matter?"

He looked up to see Kim gazing at him. "Nothing. I thought I saw a spider on the seat."

She looked down and brushed at her lap, as if that would scare a spider into running away. "I don't see anything."

"Good. Maybe it was a shadow." He put the key in the ignition and started up the car. He needed to keep his mind on his mission, which was to deliver Brianne into the loving arms of her mother. It was not to seduce the innocent baby photographer.

Annoying her was a better plan.

"So," he said, once they were driving down Bellevue again. "You were going to tell me why you changed your mind about Maine. Is it time yet?''

She leaned her head back against the seat, but her damn sunglasses hid her expression. ''It's my wedding day.''

''Excuse me?'' He wasn't sure he'd heard what he heard, but then again, there was no explaining women.

''Wedding day,'' she repeated. ''You know, dum-dum-da-dum,'' she sang. ''Dearly beloved, throw the bouquet, ride off into the sunset to live happily ever after?''

''And you gave all that up for a lobster dinner?'' He was stopped at the always interminable red light at the intersection of Memorial Boulevard and Bellevue, so he had time to study her face. There were no tears leaking out from under those dark lenses, thank God. ''I'm flattered.''

''Do your patients enjoy your sense of humor?''

''Not until after their successful surgeries.'' The light shifted so he was able to make a right turn and head toward the beach. He'd forgotten how much traffic there could be on a holiday weekend. ''So, what happened to the happily-ever-after groom?''

"He ran off with his assistant."

"Male or female?"

"Very funny. Female, of course."

"I was serious. One of the neurologists in our building—well, never mind. Is that why your sister was hovering around your apartment at dawn?"

"She wanted to keep me busy. My parents wanted me to come down to Florida and my neighbors thought that finding some bargains at the yard sales would cheer me up."

"But?" he prompted, slowing down to avoid hitting a group of bikini-clad teenagers.

"I'm not depressed. I don't miss Jeff—that's his name. Jeff. And I was a little tired of everyone trying to comfort me." She sighed. "That sounds so ungrateful, doesn't it?"

"Not really," he muttered, but he could think of a few ways to comfort her, starting with kissing and then leading to more interesting and intimate expressions of consolation. Instead he kept his mouth shut and his hands solidly gripping the steering wheel instead of reaching across the seat to give her knee a reassuring pat or take her hand.

No, he would keep his hands off. Kim Cooper

was a lethal combination of jilted bride, wholesome green-eyed goddess and sexy girl-next-door.

In other words, dangerous.

6

"COULD WE TALK ABOUT something else now?"
She should have kept her mouth shut and not
rattled on about her nonexistent wedding. She
probably sounded like a pathetic loser.

In fact, she *knew* she sounded like a pathetic
loser. This had turned into a very embarrassing
topic of conversation.

"I'm sorry about your wedding," he said, not
sounding the least bit sorry at all.

"You don't have to be. I've had a year to get
over the disappointment."

"Only disappointment? You're not heartbroken, miserable, depressed?"

"Well, I was all of those things, for a while,"
she admitted. "I thought we were going to buy
a house, have babies."

"And plant lilacs," he added.

"Yes. It sounds very naive, doesn't it."

"Everyone has a dream."

"What's yours?"

"My dream?" He was stalling. She could tell

from the way he suddenly concentrated on his driving and the view from his side mirror.

"Yes. You must have one."

"Well," he drawled, glancing over at her for a second before his gaze returned to the road ahead. "I always wanted to live in Newport. And I wanted to be a doctor."

"So far so good. What else?"

"That's about it."

"Why did you want to be a doctor?"

"I come from a long line of them. For better or worse, it runs in the family." He looked into the rearview mirror. "Bree looks like she's doing okay for now."

So, the subject had been changed. He switched on the CD player and surprised her with Frank Sinatra. Kim leaned back and looked out the window as they drove through Middletown, past a local vineyard and several flower stands. He was an excellent driver, despite the traffic. Everyone on Aquidneck Island, it seemed, was going somewhere else.

She glanced toward him once in a while. If Stuart had been sexy when scruffy, he was absolutely devastating when clean. Fresh-shaven, with a clean olive cotton shirt and dark khaki slacks, the man looked every inch the successful professional.

Kim wished she'd worn something nicer than a yellow T-shirt and black shorts. She also wished her hair was sleek and smooth instead of wispy and tousled, a cut her hairdresser had assured her would look like Meg Ryan's. Maybe she should have grown it long and gone for the Nicole Kidman style. Or super short, like her twin's trendy cut.

As if a haircut would change her life. Kim smiled to herself at the ridiculousness of that idea.

They were still south of Boston when Bree decided that life in a car seat was worth complaining about. Kim looked at her watch. Almost ten o'clock; they had been on the road for barely an hour.

She twisted around and attempted to divert the baby's attention with a stuffed elephant toy, but Bree looked at her and cried.

"Well?" Stuart turned to her and his eyebrows rose. "What do you think?"

She thought she didn't know much about babies. "She might be hungry." Or wet. Or tired of sitting in a car seat.

"I'll take the next exit," he said, which turned

on to a road that eventually led them to a Friendly's restaurant perched on the side of a rotary. Stuart turned into the parking lot and parked in the shade. "Are you hungry?"

"Actually, I am." She grabbed her purse, hopped out of the car and opened Bree's door. "I wonder if she can have ice cream."

"For breakfast?"

"It might feel good on her gums. I did a photo shoot once of a little two-year-old eating a chocolate ice cream cone. Black-and-white film, outdoors under a tree. His parents loved it."

Stuart came around to her side of the car. "Please tell me you're not going to give Bree a chocolate ice cream cone."

Kim smiled. "No, but I'm taking my camera inside with me, just in case she does anything cute."

They both moved toward the baby at the same time, bumping shoulders. Kim self-consciously stepped back at the same time Stuart did the same thing. She was uncomfortably aware of how close their bodies were, barely an inch apart as they both froze.

"Sorry. I'm in your way." He smelled a little like minty soap, something fresh and male. She had the strangest urge to lean forward and in-hale the scent of his skin, but Kim resisted. She knew better than to ask for trouble, and leaning closer to Stuart would definitely be a mistake. She started to take a step back, but his hands clasped her shoulders and held her in place.

"No," he said, his voice deep. "I kind of like you in my way."

She looked up into those dark brown eyes and saw that he wasn't teasing. He looked as if he wanted to kiss her, but that could have been wishful thinking on her part. Not that kissing him was a good idea, but it made sense to keep her mouth away from his.

Good sense.

"I'm supposed to be helping," she said.

"Yeah." And then he bent down and kissed her, which didn't help anything at all.

Oh, it helped her body come alive, because this particular kiss was not a brief "thank you" kiss or a "how are you" greeting kind of kiss. Stuart's mouth met hers with a startling warmth that shimmered along her skin and heated places in her body she'd almost forgotten existed. The straps of her shoulder bag slipped down her arm and her bag fell to the pavement before she lifted her hands and placed them, palms flat, against his chest.

Definitely a "what on earth is going on here" kiss, Kim decided through an encroaching haze of physical awareness. She could feel his heart beating under her right hand, his fingers smoothing her shoulders and then skimming down her spine to press against the small of her back.

He urged her lips apart, at the same time pressing her against the length of his body, and then he released her as quickly as he had taken her into his arms.

"Sorry," he said, setting her away from the car. "I didn't mean to do that." Then Stuart leaned inside the car and proceeded to unfasten his niece from her car seat.

Her body was still humming. She had no business humming at the edge of a Friendly's ice cream restaurant parking lot. She had no business kissing anyone in a public area in the first place.

She was supposed to be helping with the baby, not flirting with the baby's uncle. It was going to be a long day. But she'd asked for it and she had no one to blame but herself.

And maybe a set of deprived hormones screaming for release.

HE WAS TORN BETWEEN LUST and common sense.

Between politeness and desire.

Between behaving like a responsible baby-sitter or like a man who wanted only one thing: sex.

Stuart watched Kim devour two thick slices of French toast with strawberries and whipped cream while he shoved uneaten pieces of ham omelette around his plate and Brianne, safely strapped into a high chair, babbled her enthusiasm over the occasional tiny taste of vanilla ice cream mixed with a watery concoction of baby cereal.

He told himself once again that Kim was not his type, but that particular rationale was getting monotonous. She wasn't as glamorous or as sophisticated as most of the women he dated, but the green-eyed woman with the bright copper hair had her own kind of beauty.

And something told him he wouldn't have a chance with her if it wasn't for Bree.

"What kind of men do you date?"

She looked up from stirring the baby cereal. "What do you mean?"

He shrugged. "Let me guess. Divorced guys with kids, right?"

"Once."

"And?"

"He needed to spend more time with his children than with me."

"Were you hurt?"

She gave him an odd look. "That's what I told *him*. To spend more time with his kids."

"Oh." He fiddled with his coffee cup and the waitress hurried over to refill it. "So who do you go out with?"

"Why are we talking about this?" She frowned at him as the waitress dropped the check on the table, thanked them for their business and wished them a nice day.

A nice day, Stuart repeated to himself, digging out his wallet and removing a twenty. Yes, it was. And they had the whole day in front of them and there really wasn't any reason to rush. Well, there were a lot of reasons to rush, but it was more intriguing to take his time and see where the day took them.

"Let me see that map," he said to Kim. "I tucked it in the diaper bag."

She pulled it out for him and handed it across

the table. Stuart noticed it was folded neatly to the area of Massachusetts they were in.

"We're not that far from Plymouth, if we take this back road." He smiled at her and wondered if she had been as affected by that kiss as he had. "Might be less traffic, too. Have you ever seen the famous rock?"

"Once. In third grade."

"We have plenty of time to get to Payne's," he mused, eyeing the map again. He could drag out the day, bringing her home so late she couldn't go out with the accountant even if she changed her mind. "You don't mind getting home late tonight, do you?"

"Not really," she said. "Kate will just insist I go out with her if I'm home."

"Yeah. The accountant is probably washing his car right now."

"Don't tease."

"I can't help it," Stuart said, giving her the map. "I have two older sisters, remember? I was raised this way."

"That's no excuse," she told him, but he could tell she was trying not to laugh. She scooted out of the booth and started fiddling with the high chair. "I'm going to take Bree into the ladies' room and see if I can wipe the cereal from her face."

"She'll scream bloody murder," he warned, having approached the baby with a washcloth yesterday.

"She can't be dirty when we give her to her mother," Kim declared. "She'll think we— you—didn't do a good job."

"Payne has too much on her mind to worry about Bree's sticky face. So," he said, rising to help her lift the baby out of the chair. "Are we going to make a side trip to Plymouth?"

"You don't really want to see the rock, do you?"

He grinned at her. "It has its advantages. I figure the more stops we make, the more times we get out of the car and the more chances I have to kiss you."

"You're joking, right?"

"Nope. I am absolutely one-hundred-percent serious." His gaze dropped to her perfect peach-colored lips. "You have whipped cream right here." He reached out and touched the left corner of her mouth, pretending to wipe off a nonexistent spot of cream. Kim didn't look the least bit impressed. Or convinced.

"No rock," she said. "No side trips. No historical jaunts and no more—well, never mind. I'm here to help with Bree—"

"And to run away from your sister and neighbors and the blind date from hell, don't forget." He smoothed a lock of hair away from her cheek.

"—and there will be no touching, kissing or flirting." She lifted the baby and held her against her chest. "Have you ever heard of 'out of the frying pan into the fire'?"

"Meaning I'm the fire and you're an egg?"

"Precisely." She moved past him and headed down the aisle toward the rest rooms. Stuart chuckled and took a last swallow of coffee. The cute little egg didn't realize that the doctor hated to follow orders.

SHE'D NEVER SEEN ANYONE more determined to find a parking space, except for that rainy day last winter at the Warwick Mall when Kate wanted to find an open spot in front of the food court door so they wouldn't get wet.

The street that led past the fenced Plymouth Rock held bumper-to-bumper traffic, and the side streets they'd negotiated several times were lined with parked cars. But Stuart was on a mission and there was to be no talking him out of it.

Kate tried again. "You do realize that Brianne is too young to remember this."

"She's very advanced for her age." He slowed down and peered over the hood of a silver Lincoln, but the spot was taken by a motorcycle. "Damn."

"We could keep driving," she suggested, though now that they had cruised through Plymouth she realized it looked like a wonderful town to explore. The shops looked intriguing, the water across the street sparkled in the morning sun and her camera could capture it all, if she had a chance.

"No way."

"I thought you'd be happy to turn Bree over to her mother and then race home to press your tuxedo." She thought he'd be happy to return to his elegant Newport condo and his list of socialite's phone numbers.

"You forgot about our dinner. Hey, there's one." Sure enough, a car pulled out of a parking spot and Stuart took the empty space, then turned to smile at her. "I've always wanted to see this."

"Why haven't you?"

"I was brought up to be a scientist," he said, the smile dimming. "And my parents didn't have time for family trips."

"What about school? I thought every kid in Rhode Island went to Plimoth Plantation on a field trip."

"Not if you're in private school in New Hampshire," he said, then turned to look at his niece. "I hope she likes her stroller. It's one of those folding things."

"You really want to do this?" She still couldn't believe Stuart Thorpe wanted to act like a tourist and scoot his niece around town in a stroller.

He leaned over and planted a quick kiss on her lips before she had a chance to protest. "Yes, I really want to see this rock…"

"Would you please stop doing that?"

"No." He turned away and opened the door. "Come on, ladies. We're about to see where our forefathers landed."

"Your forefathers, maybe," Kim said, hopping out of the car. "Mine landed on Ellis Island."

"Another place I've never been," he said, lifting the lid of the trunk. "Too bad it's not on our way."

Kim managed to get Bree out of her car seat without much trouble. The baby only complained once, when she glimpsed her empty bottle sticking out of the top of the diaper bag, but Kim distracted her by squeaking a rubber toy. *No*, he'd said. He would not stop kissing her. She'd never felt quite so irresistible, even wearing wrinkled shorts and a stained T-shirt. Kim had learned that babies and clean clothes didn't go together. Like wealthy doctors and insecure photographers?

"UH-OH." ANNA POINTED toward Lilac House so Patrick turned to look as they drove past the old place. Two pickup trucks sat in the driveway and the front door of the house was propped open with a chair. As they got closer, Pat saw the logos on the side of the trucks.

"New England Renovation," he read aloud. "Never heard of them."

"I guess they work on Saturdays."

"It's a holiday weekend," Pat reminded her. "Kinda odd they'd be working." He pulled into Anna's driveway and parked in front of her garage, which was where they stored their eBay merchandise.

"Kimmy's not gonna like this."

"Not if they touch the lilacs, she won't." He got out of the truck and went around to help Anna, whose legs sometimes gave her trouble. "I'll unload the truck and then I'll wander over there and see what I can find out."

"I'll make us a nice breakfast," she said, taking his arm.

"We could go out." They'd decided they didn't want to leave the truck, loaded with the day's finds, sitting in a parking lot while they stopped at a restaurant. The truth was, Patrick hoped that Anna would cook for them. "My treat."

"What about what we had last night? I could eat an early lunch."

"Okay. There's plenty left over."

Which was what he hoped she'd say. Anna took a brown paper bag out of the truck. "These apples were a good deal."

"If you say so." He wouldn't have spent three dollars on a bag of artificial yellow apples, but then again, Anna had a knack for finding things that sold well. Pat looked at Lilac House again. "Maybe I'll just wander over there now and see what I can find out."

"You do that," Anna said. "Maybe Kim doesn't have anything to worry about."

He doubted that, but he kept his mouth shut. The fact that no one had bothered to answer Kim's offer to buy part of the backyard meant no one was interested in making a deal. Whoever bought the place had his own plans for the property, with or without lilacs.

Fifteen minutes later, Pat sat down at Anna's kitchen table, set the stack of mail he'd retrieved from their mailboxes on the table and eyed a torpedo roll bursting with sausages and green peppers. He was indeed a lucky man.

"Well?" Anna set down two cups of coffee and then her own plate.

"New England Renovation bought the place," he said, then took a bite of the sandwich. "That's their business, renovating houses into offices and apartments."

"And what's gonna happen to the Carlisles' house?"

"Offices on the first and second floors, an apartment on the third, one of the men told me. He even showed me the plans—they were having a lunch break and he didn't seem to mind answering questions." He took another bite of sandwich. "You could have run a restaurant, you know that?"

"I did enough cooking for my family," she

said, looking at him with a worried expression on her face. "Did you ask him about the back of the house?"

"Yeah. And it's not good."

She winced. "A parking lot?"

"Yeah," he said. He reached for the mail, unfolded the bundle and pulled out a rolled piece of paper. "It's all right here," he said, opening the paper and holding the edges flat so Anna could see. "A parking lot. Gravel, not paved, and they're putting in a new fence so the neighbors won't complain."

"Kimmy's not gonna like this," Anna muttered, shaking her head. "I wish I had a nice yard she could use."

"Yeah. Me, too." Patrick knew how she felt. He had a few spindly lilacs that had seen better days in his backyard and a couple of rhododendron bushes by his front door. He'd enjoyed growing tomatoes more than looking at bushes and, despite his large yard, he'd never been much of a gardener.

"They *gave* this to you, Patrick? Why?"

"They didn't exactly give it to me," he admitted. "I took it. *Borrowed* it." Anna looked at him as if he'd suddenly sprouted horns and a forked tail. "It was just sitting there," he said.

"Sitting where?"

"On a table on the porch. And I had the mail in my hand, so it was easy to, uh, borrow it for a while."

Anna made the sign of the cross. *"Mamma mia,"* she moaned. "You're going to go to prison. We *both* are."

"I thought I would draw a copy of this, so Kim can see, too. Don't worry, I'll bring it back when we're done looking." He eyed the landscaping plan again and knew that Kimmy was not going to be happy when she saw it.

"How are you gonna do that without getting caught?"

Pat grinned. He thought he could get used to being a criminal, though his heart was beating too fast with the excitement of it all. "I'll figure something out. Maybe you can create a distraction, the way they do in the movies."

"The only thing I create is cookies. You want some with your coffee?"

He would rather die than refuse. "Thank you, Anna. I would."

"I guess this means they don't want to sell Kim the garden." Anna stood and picked up her dirty dishes. "How are we going to tell her without breaking her heart?"

"We have all afternoon to think of something," he replied, drumming his fingers on the Formica tabletop. "Unless that fancy doctor is up to no good."

"He looked nice enough to me," Anna said, setting two mugs of coffee on the table. "If she's not gonna marry Robbie, then why not a doctor?"

Patrick didn't think this particular doctor was the marrying kind, but he kept his mouth shut.

7

BREE LOVED THE STROLLER, blinked at the sunshine, kicked her feet as if she thought she could walk, and even tolerated the cotton hat Kim found in her bag and placed on her head.

"Sunburn," Stuart said approvingly, "would not be forgiven by my sister."

"You should call her," Kim said. "Tell her where we are and how her daughter is doing."

He did, pulling the small cell phone out of his shirt pocket, but had to leave a message on his sister's voice mail when she didn't answer. "We've stopped to look at the Rock. See you later."

"That's it?"

"What should I have said?"

"Something more comforting. Leave another message so she doesn't worry."

"That's all Payne does. Worry." But he punched the redial button, waited for a moment, and left another message. "All is well," he said into the receiver. "We're strolling through Plymouth and giving your daughter a rest from the car seat and an education in the birth of the nation. She ate an excellent breakfast at Friendly's and is wearing her hat."

"There," he said, clicking the phone shut. "Did that sound comforting enough?"

"Yes." She handed him the baby, who grabbed for his earlobe and gave it a tug.

"Ouch," he said, settling Bree in the stroller. She slumped against the fabric back, but looked as if she didn't mind. "Do you think she's in there okay?"

"Looks good to me. Now you have to fix the straps so she doesn't slide out. The bottom one has to go between her legs."

He fiddled with the belt until his niece looked safe, then straightened and took the handlebars. He pointed them toward the water across the street and began to walk. "I have a very strange family, you know. We were named after movie stars," he told her. "Payne for John Payne, one of my mother's favorite actors. Temple was named for Shirley Temple, of course. And I was named for Jimmy Stewart, but my mother spelled it wrong on the birth certificate."

"This is true?" She couldn't tell when he was teasing and when he was serious.

"Yes. My mother was—is—a sweet enough woman but has the brains of a rabbit."

"That's not—"

"Nice?" he finished for her. "My mother, the beautiful Genevieve Marie Gouget Thorpe, didn't pay much attention to her children after we were born, except to tell the nanny where to buy our clothes. She is over sixty now, but prefers to be with men half her age, younger than me, I should add. She's married a few of them."

"Oh." Kim tried to picture her own mother dating a thirty-year-old man but couldn't imagine Emily Cooper doing anything remotely embarrassing, except for the time she'd walked around the house with her underpants stuck to the back of her sweater. They'd teased her about "static cling" for months.

They crossed the street when the traffic eased, then headed toward the covered area that held Plymouth Rock. "So your parents have been divorced a long time?" Kim asked.

"Yes. They sold the house in Newport years ago and went their separate ways. My father spends most of his time in Las Vegas."

"So you grew up in Newport?" She didn't know what to say to the Las Vegas remark. The vision of an older version of Stuart cavorting with glittery showgirls flashed through her brain.

"Yes. We spent summers there." He stopped the stroller in front of the fenced area and looked over the railing. "Hey, that's it."

She was surprised at how pleased he sounded. "I guess it used to be larger but people chipped pieces of it to take as souvenirs."

"I'm impressed anyway." He looked over at her and grinned. "Aren't you going to take a picture?"

"Hold Bree and I'll get you both looking down at the rock." She grabbed her camera from her shoulder bag.

"No way am I undoing that seat belt. How about if I move her over here—" he pointed to a sign that gave historical information about the site "—and we'll look enthusiastic."

"Fine." He got into position, and then Kim posed them so the light would be right. She took several quick shots, but told them to wait while she added the zoom lens. "This is for Bree's mom," she explained, focusing on the baby's chubby face. Brianne's brown eyes were wide, as if she knew she was in a place she'd never seen before. Over her shoulder, Stuart's smile was visible...and appealing.

"All set," she said, putting the camera back into her bag. "You'll be able to surprise your sister with that one."

"That will be a first," he said. "Surprising Payne has never been easy."

"You make her sound scary."

"Well," he said, obviously choosing his words carefully. "Payne's the oldest and the one in charge most of the time. She married young, to someone my parents thought was beneath her. They started their own business, now they finally have Bree and they're happy. I think Payne is determined to be the kind of mother our mother wasn't."

"And Temple?"

"Single, wild, probably hell-bent on staying away from any kind of permanent relationship. Payne worries about her."

Kim had to ask. "And what about you?"

"She worries about me, too."

"That's not what I meant."

"I like my work," he said. "And I'm not in any hurry to see if I'm smarter than my father when it comes to women. So tell me about your family. What's it like to be a twin?"

"Like having a built-in best friend," she said, following him as he guided the stroller back to the sidewalk. ''Even though we're so different, we're always there for each other.''

''And your parents? Still married and living happily ever after, I'll bet.'' She thought she heard envy in his voice.

''Yes. They sold us the business and retired to Florida. They love being outside, so the weather is perfect.'' She couldn't believe she was talking to Stuart Thorpe about the weather in Florida. She searched her brain for more interesting conversation, but sadly she had no wild relations to report. ''We have an older brother, Nick. He's a photojournalist over in Pakistan now.''

''That's pretty dangerous work.''

''He's always been the adventurous type.''

''And you?''

''*Not* the adventurous type.'' She realized they were walking toward the town. ''Are you sure we have the time to do this?''

''Sure I'm sure. My niece needs a souvenir of her first field trip.''

And then he took her hand.

Kim felt those strong fingers wrapped around hers and decided she liked the intimacy, dangerous as it was. She wanted to repeat, ''he's not my type'' over and over again in her head, but it was difficult to concentrate on reality when her hand was tucked so nicely inside his. He guided the stroller with his left hand and easily negotiated the sidewalks of Plymouth.

If she was more like Kate she would have made a joke—or not thought anything at all about such a simple gesture. But she was Kim, destined to be foolish and dream that a week from now he would remember her name.

"I'LL TAKE IT," HE TOLD the saleswoman. "It" was a stuffed bear dressed in a Pilgrim outfit. Brianne, dozing in her stroller, didn't care about bear dolls yet, but Stuart knew Payne would be thrilled. And Kim? He looked across the store to see her poking through the hat section. Stuart watched as she held up a child's white bonnet and checked the price tag. Somebody's kid was going to wear a Pilgrim's bonnet when her picture was taken next fall.

He liked her.

He wanted her. She was slender and fragile, with small high breasts and those long legs that he could almost feel wrapped around him. He was a leg man—his particular downfall when it came to women.

She picked up another bonnet, this one

smaller and trimmed with lace. Did Pilgrims wear lace, he wondered? Maybe some of the *Mayflower* passengers were fancier than others. Kim turned toward him and caught him looking at her.

"I'm done shopping," she said, but she picked up another bonnet and hesitated, as if she couldn't choose between them.

"Take your time," he said, a veteran of many shopping trips with his sisters. He paid for the bear with a credit card, signed the receipt and tucked the package into the convenient pouch that dangled from the stroller's handlebars. When he looked for Kim again she was close to him and holding both old-fashioned bonnets, which she then placed on the counter before she rummaged in her bag for her wallet.

"Let me guess," he said. "Pilgrim pictures?"

"I love to put hats on children. Even when they take them off the picture is still good. There's such surprise—oh, yes," she said, interrupted by the cashier. "I'm taking both of them."

Women who bought lace-trimmed hats didn't usually appeal to him, but Stuart decided this weekend was turning out to be a novel experience in more ways than one. He watched her without her knowing.

Seduction wasn't an option. He wished it was, but Kim Cooper wasn't the kind of woman to agree to a one-night stand. And he wasn't the kind of man who offered hearts, flowers and undying devotion. So today shouldn't be a problem. He had help with Bree, company for the long drive and even assistance with the map and road signs. So why did he hope Kim would want to spend the rest of the weekend with him?

No, sex was out. He watched as she bent down to peek at Brianne and when she looked up at Stuart she smiled.

"Shopping wears her out," he said. "Where to next?"

She glanced at her watch. "It's almost noon. Maybe we should get back in the car."

"And wake a sleeping baby? No way. Unless you want to hear her scream."

"No," Kim said, looking down at Brianne again. "I guess all that fresh air has made her feel better."

Stuart guided the stroller toward the door, which Kim opened for him. "Thanks."

"You're welcome. How far is it to Rockland?"

"I'll check the map at lunch," he promised, noticing another antique store ahead. He'd discovered that Kim liked antique stores and headed like a laser beam to vintage clothing that tended to smell like the inside of an old trunk. He did not have an ulterior motive, he told himself. It didn't matter if they arrived back in Rhode Island at midnight or even later.

It didn't matter if they had to stop and spend the night somewhere, either. Maybe one of those bed-and-breakfast places that women thought were so romantic.

"But we must be at least two hours from Maine," she said, though her attention was focused on a sign that read, Plymouth Treasures of Olde.

And another hundred and fifty miles or so to Rockland once they crossed the Maine border, he figured, though that was information he wasn't about to share. "Oh, look," he said instead, keeping his voice low so Brianne wouldn't waken. "Is that an old petticoat hanging in the window?"

"I think it's a curtain," she replied, but it was

clear from the way she stared down the street that Kim had forgotten how far it was to Maine.

He thought he should be ashamed of himself. Seduction in a New England inn was not for a woman like Kim Cooper.

But it was an intriguing fantasy nonetheless.

"I GUESS WE SHOULDN'T have stopped in Plymouth." Kim eyed the line of cars ahead of them on Route 3. They were still outside of Boston and caught in holiday traffic. She turned to Stuart, who seemed surprisingly unconcerned by the delay.

"I don't care what you say, next time I'm going to see the plantation," he said. "I can't believe you didn't want to go. We could have seen all those little Pilgrim houses and the Indian village. And I'm sure they have a gift shop."

"They do. We bought our mother a *Mayflower* refrigerator magnet." She remembered her third grade class touring the village on what had to be the coldest day of November. Kate had lost her gloves so Kim had given her one of hers.

He chuckled.

"What?"

"I'm trying to picture my mother wondering

what to do with a refrigerator magnet." He shook his head. "Sorry. Do twins run in your family?"

"According to my father, yes. The Cooper clan is famous for having twins. We even have trees planted at Twin Oaks in our honor!"

He looked over his shoulder to the back seat. "I can't imagine having two Briannes back there right now." As if she heard her name, the baby let out a loud wail of annoyance. "Uh-oh. She knows I'm talking about her and she's mad."

Kim turned around. "It's okay, honey," she crooned. "Uncle Stuart's going to stop for lunch now."

"I am?"

"Look for the 93 junction," she told him. "You're going to head west when you see the 93 sign, but we'll be in Braintree and there will have to be someplace easy to stop somewhere."

Not that Kim wanted to stop, but Brianne had eaten hours ago and should be hungry. She looked at her watch. It was almost one-thirty and they still had hours to go.

"I could eat a steak sandwich," Stuart declared. "With strawberry shortcake for dessert. How long has it been since breakfast?"

"Four hours," she said, settling back in her seat. "We left my house six and a half hours ago and we're not even in Boston yet. At this rate we won't get to Maine until next week."

He smiled. "Time flies when you're having fun."

Unfortunately that was the truth. Even sitting in traffic that should be moving three times faster than it was, she was still having fun. Stuart Thorpe had that same relaxed, confident air he'd possessed when she'd first met him. The world was all his and nothing could possibly go wrong.

Except for taking care of a teething baby. Brianne's screaming had certainly rattled him last night when he'd showed up on her doorstep. "There," she said, pointing to a sign. "We're only two miles from Braintree."

Brianne howled again, which Kim knew meant trouble.

"I'll take the first exit that has a restaurant sign," Stuart promised, slowing the car down again as traffic ahead slowed once more to a crawl. "We'll find someplace that looks good."

"We need to find a place that looks *fast*," she insisted. "Bree needs her mother and I need to go home."

"Why?"

"Because she's six months old and teething, that's—"

"No," he interrupted. "Why do you need to go home tonight? You're not going on that date, right?"

"No, but—" She was going to tell him he had the wrong idea about her, that she didn't have casual sex, that she only came along to help with the baby and run away from her family's sympathy. But she'd kissed him. And her body had reacted in a most surprising way, which actually shouldn't have surprised her at all, considering her pathetic lack of a social life.

"Yes?" he prompted. "But what?"

"I can't just *not* go home."

"Suit yourself. I'm sure we could find a historic inn overlooking the ocean somewhere near Rockland. Payne might know someplace."

"No, thanks," Kim said, trying to sound casual about the entire conversation. "I have a lot of work to do this weekend."

There were times when it wasn't easy being good.

"I CAN'T BELIEVE THIS," Anna grumbled, but Patrick noticed she managed to keep up with him as they crossed the street to Lilac House. Or what used to be known as Lilac House. A shame, really, that such a decent old house should be chopped up for offices.

"Better than tearing it down, I guess," he said aloud, surprising himself. But then again, he talked to himself all the time. Too much. If his daughter was here she'd scold him and tell him to move in with her, but Patrick had no use for California and all those cars. He didn't think his truck would last long on those Los Angeles highways.

"What?" Anna caught up with him and fanned her face with her free hand. The other held a plate of cookies.

"I'm glad they're not tearing the house down," he said, pausing in the driveway behind one of the workers' trucks.

"Betty Carlisle was a real nice woman," Anna declared. "She kept herself up, right to the end."

Patrick heard a lot of banging coming from inside the house. All the windows were open and so was the front door. Lumber was stacked in the front yard, a Dumpster sat near the driveway and on the wide front porch rolls of pink insulation wrapped in plastic were piled to the ceiling. It looked like the renovation company meant to get things done and get things done fast.

The lilacs wouldn't have much time, he figured, before they disappeared and were replaced with parked cars. Patrick's grip tightened on the seed catalogue rolled up in his fist. The landscape plans were hidden inside, waiting to be dropped somewhere when the young men's attention was focused on Anna's food.

"Hey, there," he said, when one of the young men—the tall one with the red bandanna and ponytail—stepped out onto the porch. The young man gave them a slight wave, but he clearly wasn't in the mood to visit with the old folks until Anna held up the cookie platter.

"Yoo-hoo!" She headed across the front yard. "Hello, there, young man," she called. "If you like cookies, I have something for your next coffee break."

That got his attention, Patrick saw. He knew it would. Other than a half-naked woman, nothing got a man's attention like food. And maybe a big-screen TV and a tied football game, but that would be a close third.

Yep, he thought with great satisfaction as he

followed his friend across the lawn. Anna's cooking was going to make this job easy. And after that—and maybe after a nap—he could come up with a plan to save Kimmy's lilacs.

8

"I HAVE AN IDEA."

Kim looked up from studying the road map she clutched in her hand. "What's that?"

Stuart pointed to the sign ahead. "Salem is only a few miles off the interstate. We could do another history tour. You know, witches. Sailing captains. The House of Seven Gables."

"Sister. Teething baby. Fifty miles to the Maine border."

"Where's your historical curiosity?" He wished she'd put that map away. Any minute she would calculate that after they crossed into Maine it was another two hours minimum until Rockland, Payne and turning the car around for the return trip.

"Where's your sense of time, Stuart? It's running out."

"I used to think you were shy and quiet, you know." He eased the car into the right lane.

"I am." She continued to look at the map and

her lips moved silently, as if she was counting the miles.

"I've discovered that your being the shy twin is a myth."

"Compared to Kate I am."

"I'll bet compared to Kate everyone is." He made careful note of the green and white highway signs. They'd been on the highway that skirted downtown Boston for more than an hour. In a mile or two I-95 was going to veer north. "If we go straight on 128 we would end up in Gloucester. Did you ever see the movie *The Perfect Storm?*"

"The one where the fishing boat was lost in the storm and all the men died? No."

"Me, either." When she looked up at him he added, "But I did read the book."

"How do you have the time to read? I thought doctors worked twenty hours a day."

"I'm in a practice with five other surgeons. We rotate, which is why I now have a four-day weekend." He checked his rearview mirror and then guided the car into the exit lane. It was four o'clock, which meant they could still drive through Salem and arrive in Rockland around eight, maybe earlier. Which was perfect timing for a romantic dinner and then spending the night somewhere, not that he figured he actually had a chance in hell of getting Kim to share a room with him.

"What are you doing?"

"Getting coffee," he said, wishing he could drive through Salem. He'd vacationed in Aruba, Costa Rica, Paris and Brussels, skied the Alps and even hiked along the Amazon, but he'd done little exploring in New England. "Let's spend the night in Rockland and visit Salem tomorrow, on the way back."

"I can't spend the weekend with you."

"Why not?"

"Didn't we just have this conversation a while ago?"

"That was before lunch. You've had hours to think it over."

"As if a meatball sandwich, iced tea and lemon meringue pie would make me change my mind?"

"Separate rooms," he promised. "Just two friends taking a little historical outing. Gaining a new perspective on American history."

"I was never very good at American history. Maybe you should start dating college professors from Brown instead of Newport debutantes."

He ignored the comment. "Have you always wanted to be a photographer?"

"Since I was four and my father gave us cameras for Christmas." She looked back at Bree, who started to fuss. "It's your turn to change her diaper."

He frowned. "Do you smell what I smell?"

She grinned at him and opened her window. "I certainly do."

"It's really my turn?"

"I did it before *and* after lunch, so it's your turn twice." She folded the map and tucked it into her bag as Stuart guided the car east, on the road to Salem. "Find a place to stop and I'll get the coffee while you do the, um, honor of making your niece feel more comfortable. And then we'll get right back on the road and not stop until we get to—where are we going?"

"Rockland."

"Rockland," she repeated. "We won't stop until we get to Rockland. Agreed?"

"Agreed." He hit the button to roll his window down and took a deep breath of air. The venting system wasn't enough. And, he realized, stalling too much longer wasn't in his best interest.

Handing Brianne over to her mother was.

IT SHOULD HAVE BEEN EASY to drive in and out of Salem, but after driving around in circles, negotiating traffic, and attempting to follow an array of confusing signs, Stuart decided that the local witches themselves might have designed the local roads. And he said so to Kim.

"There is no such things as witches," Kim had replied, but that was before they'd gone inside one of the buildings near the town green and saw part of a dramatic reenactment of Salem's gory past and panicked townsfolk.

"This is no place for kids," Kim had declared, and carried the baby out of the barnlike building and back into the late afternoon sunshine.

No, he thought, following her down the steps and onto a brick sidewalk. This was no place for kids. In fact, the town gave him the creeps. They'd never even come close to the House of the Seven Gables, but he'd almost been rearended twice. They'd gone around in circles, gotten lost so badly that after they'd picked up coffee to take with them—and he'd managed to change Bree's diaper without gagging—there hadn't been a chance to drink much of it.

Not that his companion seemed to mind. Taking everything in stride, Kim was definitely not shy or withdrawn or quiet. She didn't jabber on and on about things that weren't important, though. And she wasn't bitchy or opinionated or aggravating. She didn't seem to mind that her yellow T-shirt had formula smeared across the shoulder and she hadn't looked in the car's mirrored visor to put on lipstick or fix her hair.

"Were you ever a cheerleader in high school?" he asked her.

"No." She gave him a strange look and he hoped he hadn't hurt her feelings. "I was on the yearbook staff."

"The photographer?"

She shook her head. "Assistant editor. And you? Football hero and heartbreaker?"

"Science nerd. I was skinny and short until my senior year."

"I have trouble believing that," she told him, but the crowds of people walking along the sidewalk across the street caught her attention. To their left and across a busy street was a large park, green grass rolling toward a slight hill where a large brass band had gathered. It sounded as if they were warming up their instruments. "I think they're having a concert."

"Which don't you believe? The skinny part or the short part?"

"The nerd part. Let's go listen."

"Weren't you the one who wanted to go non-stop to Maine?"

"It's a band concert on a village green," she said, as if that made all the difference in the world. "Look at everyone carrying blankets and lawn chairs and coolers. It must be a Memorial Day weekend tradition."

"It's almost five-thirty now," he felt obligated to point out.

"Come on," she said, ignoring his protests. "We'll stretch our legs and get some air. Just for a few minutes."

"If one mosquito comes near Bree we're out of here," he said.

"We'll hear one song, that's all, unless there are mosquitoes," Kim agreed.

He looked back toward his car, jammed into a parking space against a hedge, near a carriage house that now advertised ice cream and cold drinks. "I've got a blanket in the trunk."

"We don't need it," Kim said, already heading toward the crosswalk. Bree snuggled against her shoulder and looked back at her uncle as if to say, "Are you coming with us or not?"

"You do realize this is going to delay that lobster dinner I promised you, don't you?" He caught up to them and took the baby out of Kim's arms. "She must be getting heavy."

"She is, but she smells good."

"I used a lot of powder." The cars stopped for a light up ahead, leaving an opening for them to cross over to the park. The band grew louder, the notes more in tune. The crowd, anxious to be entertained, applauded.

By the time they walked to the center of the park, the bandleader had announced the first song, which was "God Bless America." He invited everyone in the audience to sing along, which seemed to please Kim.

"Come on," she said, looking up at him. "Aren't you going to sing?"

"I'm tone deaf," he confessed.

"Sing anyway. I don't care." She joined in with a surprising strong soprano. Bree grabbed his ear and squealed as if she liked the music, so Stuart spent the rest of the song trying to remove his niece's little fingers from his earlobe without either one of them screaming in frustration.

"That was really nice," Kim declared, looking around the park. Out of her bag came the camera, of course, and he watched as she took several pictures of the concertgoers, then turned and took one of Bree as the band began a rendition of "You're a Grand Old Flag."

"Did she smile?"

"She likes the music," Kim said. "She's trying to sing."

"She's not trying to sing—not one of the Thorpes is genetically programmed for musical ability. She's laughing because she almost tore half my ear off."

Kim stepped closer to look. "It's red."

"Kiss me." He grinned down at her. "I dare you."

"Aren't you a little old for dares?" But he noticed she didn't move away. In fact, she leaned closer.

"Nah. I'm still the skinny kid with straight A's in science."

"Poor you," Kim said, but she didn't sound the least bit sympathetic. He didn't really expect her to kiss him, but he'd thought it was worth a try—and he'd been curious to see what she'd do.

Kim lifted her arms and took the baby out of his. "Time to go," she announced. "I hope we don't hit traffic again."

"Yeah," he said, rubbing his ear. "You'd think it was summer."

"This was fun." She began to sing along with the band as they turned away from the music, and then something went wrong. There was a crash, the music stopped and, as Stuart turned around to see what had happened, the rotund bandleader grabbed the microphone and yelled, "We need a doctor!"

"THEY NEEDED A DOCTOR," Kim explained to Payne Thorpe Johnson. She held Brianne on her hip and Stuart's cell phone against her left ear while trying to block out the sounds of the hospital waiting room. "So Stuart helped out. They think the trombone player might have had a heart attack."

"Could you tell me where you are again?"

"In Salem. Massachusetts." She winced as Brianne grabbed her hair and gave a tug. "We stopped to change Bree's diaper and get some coffee and then—just a minute." She set down the phone and untangled the baby's fingers from her hair and transferred her to her other hip. Then she picked up the phone and hoped that Stuart's sister wouldn't panic. "Okay," she said, trying to sound cheerful. "I'm back. Brianne was pulling my hair."

"And where is my daughter now?"

"Right here. She's on my lap because she was tired of the stroller. Anyway, we're here at the hospital waiting for Stuart. He wanted to make sure Mr. Whilton—"

"The trombone player," Payne supplied.

"Yes. He wanted to make sure he'd be all right and not need surgery right away. I don't think Stuart planned on doing surgery, but he did want to stay for a while."

"Excuse me," Payne said, her voice very calm.

"Yes?"

"Who are *you*?"

"I'm Kim Cooper, from Cranston. I came along to help your brother with the baby."

"Are you his girlfriend?"

"No. I'm a photographer. You hired me to take Brianne's photograph yesterday." Good heavens, she wondered. Did all of this happen only yesterday?

"Oh." Now Payne sounded happier. "The *photographer*. Cooper," she repeated. "You're the one who takes the lilac portraits. Were you able to take any outdoor portraits with Brianne and the flowers?"

"They're not quite blooming yet, but I did get some pictures of her in the lilac garden. She's a beautiful child, Mrs. Johnson."

"Payne," Stuart's sister said. "Please call me Payne. Exactly how did my brother talk you into baby-sitting?"

"It's a long story." She wasn't about to explain to Brianne's mother that she was supposed to have gotten married this weekend, that she was running away from her sister and her neighbors, that Payne's brother was as sexy as sin and twice as charming and—aside from hitting the local yard sales with Anna and Pat—she really didn't have anything better to do.

"I'm sure it is." Payne sighed. "Here's what I want you do to, Kim. Are you listening?"

"You'll have to speak up," she said. "It's very noisy in here. The loudspeaker keeps announcing things." The waiting room was also filled with people who waited to see the doctors who were on duty in the emergency room. One man looked as if he'd hit his head, another had a cut toe, while a woman held a toddler who appeared feverish. And that was just the first row.

"I want you to take Brianne out of that hospital right away," Payne said. "There are *sick* people there."

"I have to wait for your brother, Payne. I can't just drive off and leave him."

"You have the car keys?"

"Well, yes, but—"

"Then go somewhere. Anywhere. A motel. A nice, extremely clean motel. Then call me back. I'll drive down to get Bree myself tonight."

"You don't want to make that trip tonight," Kim said. "We'll bring Bree to you this evening no matter how late it is, okay?" She smiled down at the baby and prayed the little girl wouldn't fuss while her mother could hear her.

There was silence. "Payne? Mrs. Johnson?" She heard a sob and then another, meaning Payne was at the end of the proverbial rope.

"I'm sorry," she managed to say, but her voice was wobbly. "I've never been away from her before and I shouldn't have left her except my sister was supposed to take her and then bring her up here and help me because my mother-in-law's getting better, but she's still in the hospital and my father-in-law is heartbroken and has gone completely 'round the bend and my husband is frantic trying to get home from a business trip and can't deal with both of them at the same time and now Bree is in a germ-ridden environment and is sure to get sick even though she's never been sick one day in her little life and I don't know what to do." Kim heard a sob.

"It's okay. Really," she told Bree's mother. "She's been a little fussy, but I think maybe she's tired of the car. *Do* babies get tired of riding in cars?"

"Yes." Kim heard the woman take another deep breath. "Look," Payne said. "It's almost seven now. Stay in a hotel, put Bree to bed and drive up in the morning, when Stuart won't be tired."

"I don't think—"

"Please. Otherwise I'll worry about all three of you and, believe me, I don't need anything else to worry about now. Just get a motel—I'm sure you can find something nice in Salem or out on the interstate. Stuart can get a cab or something and join you later. You have no idea how long these hospital emergencies can last."

"I don't know how to find him." He had apologized, promised he'd return soon and then disappeared.

"Have him paged, tell him you talked to me

and get out of there before Bree catches something. And call me back when you're settled."

Kim agreed, clicked off the phone and looked down at the baby in her lap. "Your mommy had a lot to say," she told her. Brianne frowned and grabbed at Kim's nose.

Well, now she knew why Stuart didn't want to tangle with his oldest sister.

ANY OTHER TIME IF HE GOT a message that a woman was waiting for him in a motel, Stuart would have known it was his lucky night. One of the nurses had handed him a note, his car keys and his cell phone. The note told him where Kim had taken the baby and the black-haired receptionist at the emergency desk gave him directions.

"Your wife looked tired," the woman commented. "And the baby was starting to fuss."

"Right." His *wife*. Now there was a strange sounding word. Stuart didn't bother to enlighten the woman, but he did mention he'd call the hospital in the morning and see how the trombone player was doing.

By the time he'd found his way to the Salem Inn, Stuart was hungry and tired and needed a hot shower. He hadn't intended to spend the night in Salem—not tonight anyway, with Brianne as chaperone—but Kim must have decided the day was over, despite the fact that they had only traveled a hundred or so miles. God help them if they ever decided to drive across the country.

The building looked as if Nathaniel Hawthorne himself had slept there. The teenager at the front desk told him which room was Kim Cooper's, on the second floor at the end of a carpeted hall. She answered his knock almost immediately and put her hand over his mouth so he wouldn't make a sound.

Stuart guessed that Brianne was asleep. Sure enough, the enormous room held a lot of the baby's paraphernalia and, past a tempting wide bed and in a dark corner the baby slept in her playpen. He kissed Kim's palm, then took her wrist and removed her hand from his lips. He didn't need to deal with temptation right now, but he remembered to whisper.

"How did you get all this stuff in here?"

"The taxi driver got a big tip." Kim pushed him toward the bathroom, then shut the door so they were enclosed in the room.

"Cozy," he said, smiling down at her. Her body was only inches away from his and he considered dipping his head and placing a kiss on the side of her neck. And then he came to his senses. "Whatever possessed you to get a room in Salem?"

"I called your sister to tell her we were going to be late. Her number was in your phone."

"Let me guess. She completely freaked out over the germs in the hospital."

"Among other things. She insisted I take Brianne out of the hospital and into a hotel. At first she was going to drive down to get her tonight, but then she started crying—"

"Payne was *crying?*" He hadn't seen tears from his oldest sister since one of their father's girlfriends—Molly, he thought her name was—backed her Volvo into Payne's Mustang convertible.

"She sounded a little stressed." Kim edged closer to the door, as if she found the bathroom too confining, so Stuart moved with her. He wasn't about to let her run away.

"She always sounds stressed, but she doesn't usually cry. She usually just gets bossier." He looked around. The large bathroom was tiled in black and white, with thick towels hanging from hooks above the toilet. "This is nice. Did you get separate rooms or is that king-size bed out there mine?"

"We're sharing the bridal suite," she informed him. "Don't get any ideas. It was the last room available and it cost a fortune."

"You paid for it?" He didn't like that idea at all.

"Yes." She smiled up at him. "You owe me. Big time."

"Who gets the bed?"

"The question is, who goes shopping? We need toothbrushes, toothpaste, all sorts of overnight things. The baby's all set. Your sister packed enough baby formula and diapers to last a week."

"I'd rather talk about the bed." He watched her blush then reach for the doorknob. Teasing Kim Cooper was almost as entertaining as kissing her.

9

NEVER SEND A MAN TO DO the shopping, her mother used to say. Now Kim knew why. Stuart Thorpe had discovered Wal-Mart and had returned to the Salem Inn with four shopping bags containing his version of necessary travel items.

He was very proud of himself.

"Here," he announced, holding one plastic bag upside and dumping its contents in the middle of the bed. "Personal items and plenty of them."

Kim looked down at the pile, which consisted of enough supplies for a monthlong European cruise. "Just how long do you think we're going to be gone?"

"As long as we want," was his cheerful answer. When Bree, awake now and ready to eat again, wailed at her uncle, Stuart walked over and retrieved her from the playpen. "Uncle Stuart has a new hobby."

Kim selected a purple toothbrush. "Baby-sitting?"

"Sightseeing," he said. "Minus outdoor concerts, though."

"Is the trombone player going to be okay?"

"Probably not until after he has surgery and quits smoking, but for now, he's stable. And in good hands." He winced a little when Bree reached for his nose. "Sorry for the delay tonight. I'll make it up to you."

"You don't have to." The last thing she wanted was for him to feel obligated to her. It was bad enough to be attracted to him, to have kissed him, to have even held hands with him and thought it was wonderful.

"I had the kid at the front desk put the bill on my card," he said, turning to grab another blue Wal-Mart bag from the armchair by the bed. "And I got you some clothes. And some night things."

She was almost afraid to look, but she took the bag and set it on the bed, then peered inside. "Silk boxer shorts?"

"Oh, wrong bag." He grabbed another and tossed it on the bed. "Try that one."

She lifted out a yellow cotton nightshirt that was five sizes too big. "Well," she said. "This looks very comfortable."

"You like yellow," he said. "Right?"

"Right." She looked in the bag and then back at Stuart. "Black lace?"

"In case you were offended by cotton and preferred the Jennifer Lopez look."

"Jennifer Lopez," she repeated, taking out a long slinky gown with tiny straps. "I think the king-size bed affected your brain."

"You can't blame a guy for trying."

She chose not to comment, but she hid a smile. No one had ever bought her a black satin nightgown before and she had to admit—but only to herself—that it made her feel desirable. Almost. She reached inside and found a pair of black bikini underpants and a white T-shirt.

"The saleswoman said to keep it simple," he explained. "So I stuck with black and white and I guessed your size."

She checked the tags. A "five" on the underwear and a "medium" for the T-shirt. He'd guessed right. "You've had a lot of experience picking out ladies' underwear?"

"Don't ask. My sisters have made me shop for a lot of things I'd rather not admit to."

"Thanks for doing this," she said. "I'm glad I'm not wearing this shirt again tomorrow."

"You look fine." He smiled at her. "Do I smell pizza?"

"It came a few minutes ago." She'd been starving and had eaten a piece without waiting for him. "I started without you, but I saved you a beer."

"I noticed the cooler wasn't in the car."

"Are you kidding? Do you think I'd leave Bree's bottles behind?"

"No," he said, giving her a look she didn't know how to interpret. "You think of everything. How do you do that?"

"Do what?" By this time she had moved over to the table near the armoire and opened the pizza box. "I hope you like pepperoni."

"Take care of things." He set Bree into the playpen and gave her the pink turtle to look at.

She shrugged. "I'm the dependable type, I guess. Kate was the one who thought of exciting things to do while I followed along hoping against hope that I could prevent a disaster."

"And did you?"

"Sometimes." She lifted a piece of pizza onto a paper plate and handed it to him. "And sometimes the disasters turned into great adventures."

He smiled. "Like today?"

"Yes," she admitted. "Like today."

Unfortunately, *tonight* was still ahead.

"THIS IS A RIDICULOUS IDEA," she muttered. Not only was it ridiculous, it was totally out of character for Kim Cooper to be sharing a bed with a man she hardly knew. Well, she'd known him since college, she amended, wishing that knowing him for six years made her more comfortable with the man.

She'd left a message on Kate's voice mail after Stuart left to buy supplies. *I'm spending the night*, she'd said. And left it at that. She didn't want her twin to worry, but she didn't want to hear Kate's advice either. *Go for it*, she might say. Or worse, *I don't want you to get hurt*.

And now here she was in bed with Stuart Thorpe.

They had decided that she would get the left side and he would get the right, since she wanted to be able to see Brianne and was afraid he would sleep too soundly.

"It's a big bed," Stuart said, shifting a little under the covers. He had taken a shower and his large body was generating a lot of warmth.

Too much warmth, Kim decided.

"This is never going to work." She moved from her back to her side, then on to her back. Then on her side. Getting comfortable was impossible.

"It might, if you'd quit wriggling around like that."

"Sorry." She lay very still, on her side, facing away from him. He should have been a lot farther away than he seemed, since the king-size bed was enormous.

And way too small.

"I am not going to have sex with you." There. She'd said it, gotten the whole question right out in the open so now they could sleep.

"Sweetheart, forget about sex. I'd be happy if you would just share some of the sheet."

"I need to wrap it around me. Use the blanket if you're cold."

"We need to divide things equally," he said. She knew if she turned to look at him that she would see a tall, rangy, most excellent male body wearing nothing but boxer shorts, the silk ones.

"I usually sleep naked," he had explained. "I bought these to impress you."

She turned to look at those dark chocolate eyes of his. "It will take more than that."

He waggled his eyebrows at her, pretending to leer. "I can take them off."

"You'll look silly."

"Yes," he agreed, giving her a look that told

her he wouldn't look silly at all. "You're right. I shouldn't be lusting after the baby-sitter."

"Do not call me the baby-sitter, as if I'm some sixteen-year-old earning money to spend at the mall." With that she turned away again, facing the window and the baby's bed.

"All right. You're the sexy photographer accompanying the heart surgeon to Maine. We're about to have a sexual encounter in a romantic, historic Salem inn, while the baby sleeps like a log and doesn't wake up until nine the next morning."

"The baby rarely sleeps," she whispered, ignoring the "sexual encounter" remark. As if to agree, Brianne made a protesting noise from her makeshift bed. "She's teething, remember? That's what got me into this mess."

"Women have never called being in bed with me 'this mess' before." He rolled over and tapped her on the shoulder. "Aren't you feeling bad for hurting my feelings?"

"Go away and stay on your own side."

His fingers plucked an ample amount of material from her upper arm. "I wish you'd worn the black thing."

"I didn't want to inspire lust."

He sighed, a very loud sigh in the silence of the hotel room. Light from the street shone through the drapes and kept the room from complete darkness. "Please don't mention the word lust."

"Go to sleep, Stuart." She smiled to herself. And stayed on her side of the bed when he rolled over and settled himself in his half.

She might have known that hours later she would end up in the middle of the bed, her backside closely pressed against a warm, hard male body. Barely awake, she thought she heard a whimper but she was too comfortable to move. A large hand lay still against her breast and she thought sleepily that her bare legs and his bare legs were somehow entwined.

It was a nice dream, Kim decided, hearing her sleeping partner's light snore near her ear. No, not exactly a snore, she thought sleepily. The sound was more a groan of contentment as his fingers brushed against her breast and rubbed the cotton that covered her skin.

She was hot. And the thought flashed through her mind that she shouldn't have eaten pizza so late at night. She was dreaming again, dreams so vivid she would swear they were real except—

A baby cried.

A baby cried?

Kim tried to open her eyes and identify the

sound, but heard only silence. And felt a hand on her breast. And then she realized she was in bed with Stuart Thorpe, her backside pressed against Stuart Thorpe's almost-naked body, her breast underneath Stuart Thorpe's long fingers.

Pure heaven.

Uh-oh.

THERE WOULD BE HELL TO pay if this got out of hand.

That was Stuart's first thought when he awakened to discover Kim tucked in his arms. A lovely full breast lay underneath his hand. When he moved his fingers back and forth he felt the nipple harden, which pleased him. And made him question his sanity.

Her sweetly curved bottom was tucked against his own hardening anatomy and any minute now he would need to ease away from that delectable portion of Kim's body or have his way with her while she slept.

And she was asleep, he knew. Making love to an unconscious woman certainly defeated the purpose of making love in the first place, so Stuart lay still and inhaled the fresh scent of her hair. She'd taken a bath before bed so she smelled of rose-scented soap instead of Brianne's formula. A strand of hair tickled his chin, so he moved his head a fraction of an inch and couldn't resist kissing the delicate curve of her ear.

Brianne whimpered from the other side of the room, but Kim was asleep, he reminded himself. Even though she stirred and then stilled again. But he felt her body tense, heard her quick intake of breath, and knew she had awakened to discover herself nestled against the full length of his body.

Since she didn't scream, kick him in the groin or leap from the bed, Stuart figured he'd keep his hand on her breast and maybe nuzzle the satin sweep of skin below her ear lobe.

"Stuart," she whispered.

"What?"

"What are you doing?"

"I would think that's obvious." What was also obvious was his erection. He hoped she wouldn't be offended, but what did the woman expect in the middle of the night when they were tangled in the sheets together?

She wriggled as if she was going to move, but his leg was already over hers and stopped her from leaving. He was too sleepy and too comfortable to release her. And the wriggling only accented the problem he was having.

"Obvious? Yes."

"What do you expect when you put your, uh, bottom against my—well, you know—and wriggle around like that? I'm not exactly a eunuch." He thought she laughed, but he wasn't sure. With women you couldn't tell, but she still hadn't kicked him.

"If you would hold still—please—I'll remove my right leg and then you can take your foot off my left leg and then—"

"Shh," she hissed. "Brianne is starting to fuss."

He held perfectly still, though his fingers couldn't help moving the tiniest bit over her breast and lower, to the dip of her waist. And back up again. There was no sound coming from the playpen.

"You're supposed to be quiet," she whispered.

"I haven't said a word," he said into her ear. "I'm just getting to know you. And you feel good."

She sighed when his hand closed upon her breast again. "This isn't supposed to happen. You were supposed to stay on your own side of the bed."

"Sweetheart, we're both in the middle of the bed. This is a mutual meeting of bodies." He moved his hand down lower, skimming the rise of her hip and down her thigh to the edge of the cotton gown. "Did I ever tell you I love your legs?"

His fingers pulled the hem up her thigh and then his palm smoothed her skin.

Her hand came down and touched his wrist.

"Stuart," she said, her voice low.

"What?" He couldn't resist teasing her. "It's not as if you're wearing black silk."

"Shh," she said again and her fingers lightened. "We shouldn't be doing this."

"We're not doing anything," he said, his fingers sliding higher along her thigh as hers dropped from his wrist. "Yet."

"And we're not going to," she said, her voice quavering in the dark as his hand slid along her thigh and settled on her hip.

"I'll try to resist," he promised, wanting nothing more than to nudge her onto her back and bury himself inside her. He contented himself with stroking her thigh again, letting his fingertips drop over the curve of her leg and closer to her inner thigh.

She turned to look at him over her shoulder and he could see the shadowed curve of her cheek and lips. "I'm not good at this."

"You're not good at what?"

"Making small talk. Making love. Having sex

with men I don't know. Would you take your hand away from my leg, please?"

He did, of course. Slowly. Reluctantly. But he didn't move, relishing the feel of her body tucked so intimately against his.

That didn't last long either, because Kim scooted a few inches away and turned onto her back.

"You'll have to move over," she told him. "Or I'll fall off the bed."

Stuart moved over, but not much. He certainly didn't intend to seduce the woman, but he liked being in bed with her. He didn't think she was angry with him, not really. The woman didn't have casual sex.

He was pleased.

So pleased that he leaned over and kissed her. It was a brief kiss, and after he lifted his mouth he whispered, "Good night."

"Good night," she answered, but she looked at him as if he had surprised her again.

"What?"

She shook her head the tiniest fraction of an inch. "Nothing."

"Tell me."

"Don't you realize how strange this is or do you end up in bed with other people all the time?"

"Not *all* the time," he said, smiling down at her. "I'm kidding, Kim. I have a pretty busy work schedule. And not much of a social life, at least not these days."

"But the pictures in the paper—"

"Are events I attend for charity. A couple of my partners' wives are really into fund-raising. We all take turns going to those things." He propped his head up with his elbow. "I can't believe I'm in bed with you and discussing the last charity ball for heart disease."

"You don't expect me to believe you're lonely." She turned on her side to face him, so he quite naturally used his free hand to touch her face. She had lovely skin, and a pair of lips that would tempt a monk.

He wasn't a monk.

"No." Not lonely, not really. Bored, maybe. Tired, a little. Ready to settle down? No way. Stuart looked at Kim Cooper, sweet-smelling and soft-skinned and more vulnerable than she was aware of being, and took his hand away.

"Could you please stop looking at me like that?"

"Like what?"

"Disappointed. Surely the women you date don't end up in bed with you right away."

They usually did, he recalled. Though it had

been months since he'd had time or interest or energy to date anyone. "Of course not."

"Liar."

He smiled. "You're safe, sweetheart. I promise."

He wondered if he'd regret those words, but he didn't get a chance to find out. Brianne let out a howl that would have frightened all the so-called witches of Salem and Kim left the bed as if she'd been shot out of a cannon.

Further seduction was out of the question.

10

SHE WISHED SHE'D SPENT more time reading *Cosmopolitan*. She didn't wish she had a subscription, but those times at the beauty salon when she could have picked up the new *Cosmo* to read, she'd gone with *People* magazine instead.

And *People* magazine didn't have articles like "10 Things He Wished You Knew About His Body" or "Morning After Manners: What to Say After Hot Sex".

Kim wished she'd read something about "The Morning After No Sex" or even better, what to do when you wake up in bed next to a man who was completely out of your league, more handsome than Russell Crowe, sexier than Brad Pitt and who was wrapped around your body like a heated quilt.

The sun was shining, Brianne was sound asleep and Kim realized that once again she and Stuart were practically melded together in the middle of the bed, as if some force of nature shoved them together while they both slept.

Her foot pinned his ankle; his leg lay across her calf. She was on her side and that warm male body was tucked around hers. And there wasn't much between them aside from silk boxers and a cotton nightgown.

She hadn't worn underwear. She knew she should have last night, just for propriety's sake, but she'd never been able to stand wearing underwear to bed and she detested pajamas, too.

"You did it again," he murmured, that wonderful hand of his against her abdomen.

"Yes," she said. "I guess you must be irresistible."

"That's what all the ladies say."

"I'm sure."

"Umm." His hand moved lower on her stomach. "You're warm."

She was not only warm, but she was disintegrating underneath his palm. She hoped he couldn't tell how his touch affected her. Last night—or had it been earlier this morning—she'd managed to move away from him and, thank goodness, Brianne had cried out for half a bottle and some comforting medicine on her gums. But now...well, now Kim wanted only to feel those fingers of his caress her skin, pull up her nightgown and have his way with her.

She thought she should be stronger early in

the morning, but she'd never really been a morning person. And the few times she'd awakened next to her fiancé, he'd hopped out of bed ready to begin the day.

What Stuart seemed ready to begin was different, because his fingers caressed her, though carefully keeping away from her breasts as if he was afraid she would demand he move away again.

"Hold still," he whispered close to her ear. "I'm only going to touch you." His hand dropped lower, a featherlight touch against her inner thigh. He drew up the hem of her gown with aching slowness, sending frissons of awareness along her skin. Heat pooled between her legs as the most intimate places of her body were exposed to the air.

"Stuart."

"Shh." His lips found her shoulder where the large nightgown had slipped and exposed skin. She turned her head and he kissed her mouth.

And she was lost, floating on a sea of sensation that made her forget that she wasn't an adventurous or sensuous person. Right now, parting her lips for Stuart's tongue, she'd forgotten she'd been lost in Salem. For now Rhode Island and the lilacs seemed very far away.

And not part of her life at all.

His fingers found her, touched and teased and caressed with aching slowness and tender skill. The nightgown was a tangle of material above her waist, her body twisted toward him so her hand could feel the warmth of his neck. Her last rational thought was that she had never felt so completely undone before, or quite so reckless.

He had that effect on her.

His finger entered her, slid and delved with tantalizing motions. One finger, then two, and she moaned against his mouth as she spiraled out of control. His thumb skimmed over the most sensitive nub, then returned to send heat spinning through her until breathing was impossible—along with any attempt to control the intense reaction of her body to his touch.

Her breath mingled with his when she came against his hand.

But when he released her lips, withdrew his fingers and would have moved above her to join his body with hers, Brianne—like any good chaperone—let out a shriek of indignation that stopped passion cold.

"Bad timing," Stuart muttered, sprinkling kisses down Kim's throat.

Or not, she thought, wafting slowly back to

earth. There was such a thing as too much intimacy, as moving too fast and being completely out of control.

There was such a thing as being a spineless, wanton fool who couldn't resist sleepy morning lovemaking.

"Maybe it's for the best," she said, attempting to move out of his arms. Brianne continued to shriek.

"Easy for you to say," he said, smiling down at her. "You're blushing."

"I do that."

"After making love?" He nuzzled her neck.

"After talking about it. Are you always so…uninhibited?"

"The human body," he said, lifting his head to look down into her eyes, "is a wonderful and magic piece of equipment."

"Equipment," she repeated, wondering if that was flattering or not.

"And your…equipment is absolutely enticing." He kissed her nose before moving away. "I'll get the baby. You get the shower. Deal?"

"Deal."

Though she would need more than hot water to wash away the memory of the past few moments.

SHE WORE HER BLACK shorts and the new white T-shirt he'd bought for her. Once again the sight of those long legs of hers drove him crazy. He went hard just thinking about how those legs felt alongside his in bed this morning.

"We're just a few miles away from Brunswick," Kim said, her attention on the map folded across her lap. "That's where we should turn off."

"Yes." He'd looked at the map this morning, while he held Bree and listened to Kim taking a shower. He'd wished he could join her, but instead he'd fed his niece, changed her diaper and tucked her into a new outfit so her mother would know she'd been well taken care of. Bree had drooled and gurgled and grabbed his chin.

"It looks like it's sixty-four miles to Rockland," Kim informed him. "If I counted correctly."

He didn't want to talk about maps or miles or Maine. He wanted to ask her if she would spend the night with him tonight. Somewhere overlooking the ocean, which shouldn't be too difficult to find here on the coast.

Somewhere without a baby to care for, which should be easy. Once Payne took her baby into her arms there would be no question of anyone else baby-sitting for a long while.

Somewhere romantic, where he could order champagne.

And somewhere with no telephones, hyperventilating trombonists, outdoor concerts, or witch museums. He wanted Kim Cooper's full attention tonight.

He wanted to make her come again. And again. So he could watch her blush afterward and he could cover her body with kisses and tease her until she laughed, until her shyness evaporated and was replaced by passion. He wanted to ease himself inside of her and make love to her for a long, long time.

Until they were sated and replete and could barely catch their breath.

Stuart shifted in his seat and tried to keep his mind on the traffic, of which there was little.

"I've never been to Maine. Have you?"

He glanced over to see her looking at him. If he hadn't been driving, he would have leaned over and kissed her. She made him want to do that. It was odd, this feeling. He wasn't usually affected by women this way. "Not this part of Maine, no."

"There aren't any museums or historical sites you want to see before we get to Rockland, is there?"

It took a second or two for him to realize she was teasing him. "The only thing I want to see is my brother-in-law's family home."

"And your sister," she added. "She wasn't upset this morning, was she?"

He thought about his phone call to Payne after breakfast at a little café by the interstate. "No. Her mother-in-law's condition has improved. And she can't wait to see Bree. Temple called and begged forgiveness for being stuck in Mexico and promised to make it up to her."

"What was Temple doing in Mexico?"

"She has an investment and design business. She was either on vacation or buying pots." He didn't want to talk about his family. He wanted to talk about tonight. "Do you like islands?"

"What kind of islands?" She was looking at the map again.

Islands where no babies cry and disturb lovemaking couples.

"We could stay on one of the islands in Penobscot Bay for the rest of the weekend. If you like."

He met her gaze. She had the most amazing green eyes.

"We just passed a sign for the Maine Maritime Museum," she said. "It might not be as exciting as Plymouth Rock, but we could stop on the way home."

"Is that a yes or a no?"

She held up one of the brochures she'd collected when they'd stopped for gas in Portland. "There's also the Farnsworth Art Museum. Or Penobscot Marine Museum and the Belfast and Moosehead Lake Railroad."

"Very funny. I'm talking about a romantic weekend and you're acting like a tourist."

"You liked being a tourist yesterday."

"I was trying to stall so we would have to spend the night together."

"And we did."

"With a screaming chaperone," he pointed out. "Who has a terrible sense of timing." He checked his rearview mirror to see Bree sound asleep in her car seat.

"We also have the Marshall Point Lighthouse Museum and the Owls Head Transportation Museum. They have a 'classic 1937 Mercedes,'" she read.

"Really?" Then he caught himself. "We have better things to do with our weekend," he insisted.

Kim was blushing again. Stuart decided that was a good sign. He didn't know how it had happened, but in the past forty-eight hours his life had changed. Oh, it was lust, pure and simple. He wasn't the kind to fall in love and toss moonbeams at his beloved's feet, but this woman was special.

He wasn't falling in love with her, of course. Stuart Thorpe didn't do things like that.

"SHE DOESN'T DO THINGS like that. Something's wrong. Kim wouldn't go off and not come home."

"You think?" Anna turned down the heat under the pot of meatballs and sauce and poured two cups of coffee.

"Yeah, I sure as heck do." Patrick was at wit's end, having woken up early Sunday morning certain that his young neighbor would be home. He'd waited patiently until after ten o'clock before walking over to knock on her door. He was sure she'd want the latest news on the Lilac House once she noticed that there was work being done.

"He is a very handsome man, that doctor is." Anna set a cup of coffee in front of him. "Here. Drink up. I'm making meatballs for later. We'll have a nice sandwich together."

Even the thought of Anna's special meatballs couldn't cheer him. "I told you I didn't trust that fancy doctor with the fancy car."

"It's a long way to Maine and a long way back," she insisted. "She could be gone all weekend."

"And the lilacs? What will she say when the lilacs are gone?" She would think her friends had let her down. He didn't know what was worse, Kim losing her lilacs or her faith in her neighbors.

Anna sighed, reached into the pocket of her apron and pulled out a tissue. "She's not gonna be happy," she replied, wiping her eyes.

"We've got to warn her. Katie will know where her sister is, won't she? Let's call her." Which meant Anna should call her. Woman to woman and all that.

"Okay. I got her number here somewhere." Anna searched through the papers stacked on the counter, then dialed her phone.

Patrick fixed his coffee with milk and sugar and tried to interpret Anna's conversation with the wild twin. Now Katie, there was one who got into trouble. No wonder her parents moved to Florida. They'd probably gotten tired of worrying about her antics.

"Well?" Patrick watched Anna hang up her phone and then head over to the stove to stir her meatballs. "What did she say?"

"Kim called her this morning and said there was an emergency—"

Patrick didn't like the sound of that, not one bit. "What kind of emergency?"

"Dr. Thorpe had to help someone so they ended up getting to Maine later than they planned. She won't be back until today, or later if they stay and help Dr. Thorpe's sister with the baby." She wiped her wet hands on a towel and hung it by the sink. "Kate didn't talk to her because she wasn't home. That was the message on her machine."

"The guy in charge yesterday—the one with the red bandanna—said they were going to get a dozer over there either tomorrow or Tuesday. He didn't know for sure, with it being a holiday weekend and all."

"What are we gonna do?"

"You're not going to like it, Anna."

Her big brown eyes widened. "You're not going to steal a bulldozer, are you?"

Patrick stared at her. "You're a genius, my friend. As well as a gourmet cook."

She laughed and waved the wooden spoon at him. "I never know when you're kidding."

He wasn't kidding. In fact, he wondered where he'd stored the box of military souvenirs they'd bought last week. In the garage, most likely. He'd get the ladder after lunch.

There were times when a man had to plan for the worst-case scenario.

"THANK YOU AGAIN," Payne Johnson said, holding her daughter close to her. "I don't know what my brother would have done without you."

"You're very welcome. I hope she gets her new tooth soon." Stuart's oldest sister looked very much like him; she was tall, with dark hair and eyes and a quick smile. There were dark shadows under her eyes and she looked worried, though she'd explained that her mother-in-law had surprised them and was improving, and Phil had arrived from the Portland Airport earlier this morning. She'd fixed them lunch, though Stuart had tried to prevent her from fussing.

Kim wondered if all three siblings were equally stubborn.

"And the photos? Do you think they came out well?"

It took Kim a moment to remember Friday's session. "I haven't developed them yet, but Bree was a good subject and behaved herself."

"She's lying." Stuart opened the passenger

door. "Bree threw several temper tantrums and gave us all a hard time. She reminds me of her mother, you know?"

"Don't try to annoy me, little brother. I have my ways of getting even."

"Not today, you won't," he said, giving Kim a pleading look. "We've got a long drive ahead of us and we're getting out of here."

"You're welcome to stay," Payne offered once again. "It's a large house with plenty of room. And you could see Rockland. If you like pottery there's a wonderful—"

"Payne," Stuart interrupted. "Stop. I will take Kim into Rockland and let her roam the shops if she wants."

"You should bring Kim back this summer for the lobster festival." She turned to Kim. "Phil and I come up every year for that. He grew up in Rhode Island but his parents moved to Rockland years ago."

"Payne," her brother said again. "It's after three o'clock and your daughter needs a nap."

"All of a sudden you're an expert on babies?" She laughed, but stepped back and let Kim climb into the car.

"I've had no choice," he insisted. "And I didn't do too badly, either."

"You had help. We'll see you again." Payne gave Kim's shoulder a light pat. "With him or without him."

"I'll call when the proofs are ready," Kim promised. And in a few minutes they were driving away, heading down State Street and away from the Johnsons' two-story cottage.

"Now," Stuart said, once he had guided the car back onto Main Street. "Please don't tell me you want to go home."

When she hesitated, he smiled. "What about the lighthouse museums and the antique autos and all that?"

"You really don't want to do that."

"No. I want to get a room with a bed and make love to you for the next twenty-four hours."

"I don't think anyone's ever said that to me before." She'd had her share of offers, but nothing so forthright. Or so tantalizing.

"You're kidding."

"Well," she said. "Mrs. Gianetto's nephew offered a weekend in the Poconos with a heart-shaped bed and a private hot tub."

"Did you resist?"

"I did." Resisting Robbie had been easy. But saying no to Stuart Thorpe was just about impossible. And yet...saying yes seemed absolutely foolish. He was a heartbreaker, a flirt, a man guaranteed to break her silly heart. "Could I think about it?"

"Sure." They were at a stop sign. "I'm going to go right here on 73 and end up at a place called Craignair."

"What is it?"

"An inn. There's a brochure in that pile of tourist stuff by your feet." She reached down and picked up the papers. "It's on someplace called Clark Island."

"Do we have to take a ferry?"

"No. It's at the end of Clark Island Road, on a cliff that overlooks the ocean."

"I suppose you already made reservations." What else would he think, after she'd snuggled up to him in bed last night and then allowed him to… Her face grew hot just thinking about it.

"I called to see if they had any rooms and they had plenty. I didn't make a reservation, Kim. But I thought it looked like the kind of place you would enjoy."

Enjoy? He didn't know the half of it. Falling in love with Stuart Thorpe was the stupidest thing she had ever done.

Concealing it would be the smartest.

11

THEY TOOK THEIR TIME, driving through the small coastal towns of South Thomason and Spruce Head, stopping for clam chowder and then to purchase sweatshirts, as the wind had turned brisk, despite the sun. By the time Stuart took the turn down Clark Island Road, Kim knew that soon there'd be no turning back. She either had to follow her heart or ask Stuart to turn the car toward Rhode Island and plan to spend the rest of the weekend alone.

This wasn't going to be easy.

"If you want to stay here, at the inn, we could get a room with twin beds," he offered. "Or we could get two rooms, and meet for breakfast in the dining room and watch the ocean while we wake up. Either way, the place looks interesting."

Interesting? They'd come upon a spectacular three-story white inn perched on the edge of the water. It wasn't intimidating or elegant—the brochure said it had originally been a boarding house—but it looked comfortable and quiet and exactly right for a romantic evening.

"Or we could drive home tonight," he offered. "We'd probably be back by eleven or so."

"This is all so easy for you."

His eyebrows rose as he turned toward her, the car engine still running. "Easy? In what way?"

"You're very comfortable with all this."

"All this?"

"Sex. Weekend vacations. Romantic inns."

"Teething babies, worried sisters, wrong turns—" His mouth descended on hers for a leisurely, searing kiss.

"We were only lost a few times," she interjected, hoping to catch her breath and try to think clearly.

"I'm also good at hospital emergencies, buying new underwear and eating cold pizza."

"I offered to try to heat it up with the hair dryer."

"You can't convince me that would have worked."

"I still think it would have," she insisted, before he kissed her again. She looped her arms around his neck and for a long moment forgot where she was and what she was supposed to be thinking about. *Maine*, she reminded herself, after he'd lifted his lips from hers. *I'm in Maine and I should go home.*

To an empty bed and a darkroom full of work?

Somehow that wasn't at all as appealing as spending the night making love with Stuart Thorpe.

"While you're deciding about the rest of the weekend, we could walk around the grounds. It's a little cold for flowers but maybe you could find something to take pictures of."

He parked the car and opened the door, then came around to her side of the car. Kim hopped out into the wind and brushed her hair back from her face.

Oh, Lord, he was handsome. He wore his new black polo shirt and yesterday's khaki slacks, but he looked like someone who had stepped out of a magazine. His dark hair was windblown and wavy, his mouth smiled easily. She wondered if all of his female patients were in love with him.

She wanted to say yes, wanted nothing more than to have the adventure of her life, to have the kind of weekend that Kate would enjoy so freely. She wanted the kind of weekend that would make her smile when she was an old woman.

A romantic night at an inn in Maine, along the coast, with a laughing man who touched her with such tenderness she had to hold her breath when she remembered how exciting it had been.

"We should also go out for lobster," he added, holding out his hand to her. "I haven't forgotten that dinner I promised."

What he promised was hot passion and the amazing feeling of being desirable and not just plain old Kim Cooper, children's photographer and the "quiet" twin.

"Then I think you should keep your promise," she declared, taking the warm hand he offered. "So we should stay."

"I would like that," he said, his voice low.

"Me, too." Today, tonight and tomorrow she would enjoy herself. Kate would warn her about getting hurt, but Kim thought she could take care of herself, at least for the next day or two.

A romance with Stuart Thorpe certainly wouldn't last much longer.

THAT EVENING KIM WORE the black gown, but she laughed a little as she crossed the large expanse of carpet between the bathroom and the wing chair by the window where Stuart sat gazing at her.

"I don't feel at all like myself," Kim admitted, standing in the shadow away from the lamplight.

"It is a little different from the cotton thing you wore last night," he said, his mouth dry.

"A few days ago the only thing I worried about was how to buy the lilac garden. Now look at me."

He was looking, all right. He was constantly amazed at how beautiful she was, and he was once again surprised at himself for not realizing her beauty when he'd met her years before.

He was an idiot, a fool who deserved to be nervous.

Kim lifted her glass of white wine from the table and took a sip as she looked around the room. She seem pleased enough with the place. The brochure hadn't lied; the pale green room was filled with antiques, and the queen-size bed was a four-poster topped with carved wooden pineapples. A wide window faced the sea and its gold and green damask drapes would block out the night when pulled shut.

There was a private bathroom, done in white and mint green, with a huge claw-foot tub that Stuart suspected could hold two people.

He was willing to try, but he had to live through the night first.

"You're happy with the inn?" Their hosts had been pleased to see them, apologized for the cool afternoon breeze and the state of the gardens. There had only been one other couple in the downstairs parlor, so only two of the inn's thirteen rooms were occupied.

It was as if they had the place to themselves.

"Yes. It's old and cozy and not at all intimidating. It's perfect."

He was suddenly very glad she didn't marry that other guy. That bastard had to be the dumbest man on the planet.

"You're frowning. What's the matter?"

Stuart didn't know what to reply. "I think," he said, hesitating a little, "you take my breath away."

"You? Mr. Newport Rhode Island bachelor?" Her green eyes tilted up slightly when she smiled. "I don't believe you."

"Oh, believe it," he said, taking her hand. Her fingers were small and elegant, with short unpolished nails. He wanted to feel those fingers on his body, but he told himself to take it slow. They had all night.

"I'll try."

"Do you know this is the third night in a row we've spent together?"

She laughed. "It's been quite a weekend."

And then she blushed a little, and the sight made his groin harden more than he thought possible. He shifted a little on the chair and pulled Kim carefully onto his lap.

"Our chaperone isn't here this time."

"No." Her arm went around his neck. "And we're nowhere near any museums or places of historical significance."

"Except the bed." He smoothed his hand over the silk covering her thigh. He'd thought about those thighs all day.

"And I've had my lobster," she added.

"A lobster salad roll isn't exactly a gourmet dinner, sweetheart." He couldn't believe she'd been pleased with takeout tonight from a place called "The Lobster Shack," but Kim Cooper was different from any other woman he'd ever met.

Stuart knew he should be terrified. He should be running like hell, instead of running his fingers along the woman's leg. Kim took another sip of her wine and leaned forward to set the glass on the nearby table. Her breasts brushed his arm, which was almost his undoing. She also switched off the lamp, which happened to be the only light in the room aside from the moonlight coming in the window.

"It was the best lobster roll I've ever had," she declared. "And the fries weren't too bad either." She leaned back and snuggled into his arms, then touched his shirt. "Why are you still dressed?"

"I thought I'd give you a chance to change your mind." Which would, of course, have sent him leaping from the second-story window. He would have howled his disappointment into the night as he fell.

"This morning—" She stopped, but he couldn't see her expression.

"This morning?" he urged. He dipped his hand under the hem of her gown and slid his hand over her knee. She was warm satin and she shivered when his hand moved higher and his fingers slowly touched her inner thigh.

"I've never—you have magic hands."

"Your body opens for me," he said, touching her petaled folds already slick with passion. "That's magic."

"It all is, isn't it?" She quivered again as he touched her, played with her, memorized the feel of her arousal against his fingertips. She was delicate and small and luscious, and he knew if he didn't get her to bed soon he was going to embarrass himself.

Stuart took a deep breath, counted to five and, intending to remove his hand and carry Kim to bed, decided to stay right where he was, at least until he'd undressed her—and himself. Besides, he didn't know if his knees would hold him up, because at the moment he was feeling more than a little shaken.

And about to explode.

"What about you?" she asked, her voice very soft in the darkness. "Your clothes—"

"Will come off now." He couldn't wait any longer. He lifted her from his lap and set her on her feet. Then he stood and began to remove his shirt, with Kim's soft fingers trying to help. He tossed his shirt to the floor and was about to reach for his pants when Kim surprised the hell out of him. Her fingers skimmed the waistband of his slacks and with her index finger she traced the outline of his sex.

It was almost enough to send him over the edge.

"You have magic hands, too," he said, echoing her words. But he couldn't last much longer with her hand anywhere near him, so he took her wrist and guided her hand to his chest while he removed the rest of his clothes.

He didn't know how they made it across the room to that wide, welcoming bed. She smelled like roses and felt like silk when he removed the ebony gown and sent it spinning to the carpet.

This time when he cupped her breasts he was awake and aware that his touch pleased her. This time when they fell into bed together it wasn't with the understanding that they would stay on their own sides.

And this time, when he moved over her body and kissed her, it was with the knowledge that he would soon be inside of her, would make love to her for as long as they both wanted, for as many times as each of them needed.

Until they'd each had enough of lovemaking and wanted to sleep. Stuart didn't think he'd want to sleep, not with Kim in his bed.

He remembered the condom, then put himself against her and moved his hips enough to penetrate her softness, to test her body and give her time to accept him.

But she moved, urging him closer, so he went

deeper. She fit around him perfectly. Tight and wet and hot, with thighs like satin and with welcoming hands on his backside, she urged him deeper, took him inside her and asked for more.

He stilled, looked down into her oval face and saw surprise in her eyes. "Kim?"

"Yes?" Her voice was a mere whisper.

"Are you all right?" He thought he would die if she said no.

"I think," she said, looking at him with those slanted green eyes, "it's perfect."

"Perfect," he repeated, pleased she thought the same as he did, moving inside of her to test the feeling.

"Magic, even." She smiled, so he dropped a kiss on her mouth.

"Don't stop," he heard her say when he lifted his lips from hers.

"No," Stuart promised, knowing it would be impossible to keep still a second longer. Even the slightest motion made him ache. "Stopping would be impossible."

"I'm glad."

Yes, that's what he thought, too. And so he made love to her, moving deep inside of her with even strokes. It lasted forever; it was over too soon. He managed to keep control until Kim lost hers, as her breath came faster and then she climaxed, contracting around him as if a velvet hand had him in her grasp. He closed his eyes and, with a force that seemed out of the ordinary, the deep ache at the base of his penis burst into a climax of dizzying proportions. He made no sound, but grit his teeth and hoped he wasn't hurting her.

When it was over, when he could finally remember to breathe, Stuart opened his eyes and looked down into the face of the woman who'd so obviously taken his heart.

She was smiling.

He thought he might have fallen in love with her.

And broke out into a cold sweat.

"WILL WE DROWN?" Kim leaned back in the bath and eyed the naked man who was about to climb into the tub. She loved looking at his body, all angles and planes and muscle.

"Not unless you do exactly as I say," he said, pretending to leer as the warm water rose over her breasts.

"I'm not sure I like the sound of that," she replied, bending her knees to give him room. She couldn't quite believe the past fourteen hours. They'd made love twice since the first time, slept late this morning and now, as they readied themselves for the drive home, it turned out they couldn't keep their hands off each other.

Even taking a bath in the huge old tub was turning into an erotic experience.

"Spread your legs," he said, and when she dropped the soap and followed his instructions, he lifted her onto his lap. His erection bobbed against her, so she reached beneath the hot water and stroked it.

She heard him groan and was thoroughly pleased with herself.

"Now," he said, lifting her onto him. She came down slowly, with him hot and hard inside of her. Kim gripped Stuart's bare shoulders and felt the water splash against her spine.

The motion was leisurely now, the water soothing as it rippled around them. He reached down below the water and touched her where they were joined, knowing now where she was the most sensitive and how to bring her pleasure. Kim felt herself tensing, building to a peak as heat centered and pooled and finally burst deep within her, where his stroking had increased in speed and force. She felt him come within her, his lips found her neck and when it was over Kim wondered if she would ever be the same again.

Surely her body would remember this for a long time to come, while her heart had better forget making love with Stuart Thorpe had ever happened.

"NOPE, STILL NOT HOME." Patrick paced back and forth in front of the bay windows that faced the photography studio across the street. The place looked empty; there were no lights on, no windows open and Kim's car was still in its spot in the driveway.

In contrast, the bustling workers at Lilac House were still swarming around the place like ants around a picnic. Patrick figured they must work by the job and not by the hour, considering they looked like a group of men who didn't like to waste time. They were picking up tools now, stacking supplies on the porch and loading their trucks.

"She must be having a nice time."

"Humph." He didn't want to think about what "nice time" described.

"Come sit down and watch the news with me." Anna eased herself into her flowered recliner and tilted it back a notch. She adjusted the volume of the television with the remote control and found a channel worth watching. "I'm glad you talked me into getting one of those satellite dishes."

"Think she'll have time to take some pictures tomorrow?" Patrick sat on the couch and eyed the television screen. Anna watched the damnedest things, but that Animal Planet station was the worst. Right now there was that idiot who wrestled alligators. In fact, Patrick figured that every other time Anna clicked on that channel, that same guy was fooling around with the exact same alligator, only in a different pond.

"She might. If we're not in jail. And if she isn't too tired."

"She's twenty-six," he pointed out, ignoring the reference to jail. "What could she have to be tired about? Those Cooper girls have always had the energy of a dozen kids, don't you remember?"

Anna turned toward him and shook her head. "Mercy me, Patrick, you're turning into a grump. Didn't you and your wife ever go on romantic weekends together?"

"We were married," he grumbled. They'd

both been virgins on their wedding night, even. Not that he wanted to share that piece of information with his neighbor. "It's different."

"Not so much, I don't think."

"I don't want to talk about this."

"Then watch television for a while," she said. "I've got the cooler all packed and ready to go. And you filled the water jugs. What else do we need?"

"Nothing. They'll be bringing the dozer first thing in the morning, so don't forget to set your alarm for five."

"I won't," she promised. "I'll probably be awake before then anyway. I hope this works."

"It'll buy Kimmy some time," he declared, turning to look out the window again, but the house across the street was still dark. "I hope she gets home soon."

"Yes," Anna sighed. "We're gonna need someone to post bail."

12

THE SIGHT THAT GREETED Kim Cooper Tuesday morning was something she could never have imagined at seven o'clock in the morning. Several cars were parked in front of the studio, including her sister's. The driveway of Lilac House was filled with pickup trucks, and a small group of construction workers huddled around a bulldozer in the front yard.

"Stuart, slow down," she cried, realizing there was a crowd gathered in the photo studio's parking area. "It looks like they're going to tear down Lilac House."

One of the people gathered in the driveway turned a worried face toward the Mercedes. Kate's expression shifted to relief as she recognized her twin and hurried toward them. Stuart parked the car in front of the house.

Kim grabbed her bag and was out of the car in a flash. "Kate? What's going on?"

"Where have you been?"

"We stayed in Newport last night, at Stuart's

condo," she said. And what a night it had been. She had a lot to tell Kate, but her sister didn't look as if she was pleased with Kim's sudden decision to go off with Stuart instead of a blind date with the accountant Kate had chosen.

"I've been leaving messages—oh, hello, Stuart. Where the hell have you two been?"

"Maine," he said, his attention taken by something behind Kate. "What's happening in the backyard?"

"You have to see for yourself," Kate declared. "Come on, Kim. Let's see if you can talk some sense into them." She led them toward the back of the studio, past a handful of curious neighbors and a couple of high school students.

"Them? Is someone going to destroy the lilac garden?" She felt tears spring to her eyes at the thought of losing such a special place. "Don't they know how old those bushes are? And what are they doing to the house?"

"The house is being converted into offices and apartments," Kate said. "That's what Patrick told me. He and Anna have been talking to the workmen and have seen the plans. The backyard is being turned into parking."

"And the lilacs?" She wondered if it was too late to try to dig them up.

"See for yourself." Kate waved her arm toward the garden.

Anna and Patrick waved back. They were in lawn chairs placed at the outer edge of the bushes; beside their green and yellow metal chairs was a bright red plastic cooler, two jugs of water and a thermos.

"What are they doing?"

"They've handcuffed themselves to the lilacs," Kate explained. "They've been waiting for you."

"Oh, Lord."

"Handcuffs?" Stuart strode across the lawn, with Kim and Kate trying to keep up.

"Hey, there, Kimmy!" Patrick broke into a huge grin. "You're just in time!"

"In time for what, Patrick?"

"To keep us out of prison," Anna answered. She reached into a tote bag and pulled out a bag of anise cookies. "Here. I brought some for you. You, too, Dr. Thorpe. Help yourself."

"Anna," Kim said. "No one's going to put you in prison."

"I am," a burly, dark-haired construction worker declared. He stood next to Kim and folded his hands across his chest as he frowned at her. "Are you in on this, too?"

"He's cute," Kate whispered, giving the man one of her dazzling smiles.

"Hey," he murmured appreciatively. "There's two of you."

"Cute *and* smart," Kate replied, while Kim elbowed her to keep quiet.

"I just got home—" she told the man.

"And it's about time, too," Patrick added. "We couldn't let your lilacs get bulldozed, Kimmy, so we decided to have a sit-in."

"A sit-in?" They were in their eighties. It was seven o'clock in the morning. They weren't protesting a war, but preventing a demolition. Kim supposed somehow it all made sense, but she didn't know how.

Patrick shook his head as if he couldn't believe she didn't understand what he was up to. "I guess you're too young to know about the sixties. That's all those kids did then, you know, have sit-ins and smoke pot."

"*Who's* smoking pot?" someone in the crowd asked.

"You've got to get them out of here," another worker said. This one sported a blond moustache and wore a red bandanna around his forehead. "And as soon as possible. Do you have any idea how much it cost to get a dozer operator in here?"

"Do you have any idea how gorgeous these lilacs are?" Kim put her hands on her hips.

"We're putting in a new drain system, honey. And a parking area for the tenants. I've got my orders."

"You're not the owner of the house?"

"No. I work for—hey, get that dog out of here!" A neighbor's black Labrador picked that moment to lift his leg on a plastic-covered pile of lumber. The crowd tittered and a couple of people applauded.

Stuart took a step backward. She heard him say something about "phone calls," "rounds," "surgery" and "sorry," but she didn't have a chance to turn around and talk to him. Anna handed her the bag of cookies and Patrick muttered something about not being too old to show these young men a thing or two about getting a job done, at the same time fiddling with his hearing aid.

"Kim, dear," Anna said. "Would you keep Patrick company while I go to the bathroom?"

"Sure."

"*Sure?*" Bandanna Man did not look pleased. "Lady, get these people out of here before I call the police and never mind about bathroom breaks. We've got *work* to do."

Meanwhile Kate stood whispering with the dark-haired worker. Then she tugged on Kim's sleeve. "There's something you should know, I think."

"I really have to go," Anna insisted. "All this coffee and excitement..."

"Just a minute." Patrick fished a key out of his jacket pocket and unlocked Anna's cuff. "Hurry back. It looks like we're making headway here."

Anna winked at Kim, who helped her out of the wobbly metal chair. "Pat's so glad you're back. He's been fretting over these bushes all weekend."

"There's nothing we can do to stop this," Kim told her as they headed toward the back door of the studio. "Though it was so wonderful of you two to try."

"Well," the old woman sighed. "I hated to see you come home and find the lilacs gone. I know how much you enjoy the garden."

"Yes, but it's not worth you or Patrick getting hurt."

She laughed. "They're not going to attack two old folks, Kimmy."

Kim opened the door for her and Anna, who knew the layout of the studio, hurried inside. Kim waited at the foot of the steps and saw Stuart's Mercedes drive down the street.

He hadn't said goodbye, or maybe he had and she hadn't heard him. Her things were still in his car, but she didn't think she'd have much use for a black satin nightgown in the future. She'd had a romantic, sex-filled weekend with one of the handsomest men on the planet. She'd escaped the pity of her friends and family. She'd seen Plymouth Rock.

And she had known all along it wasn't going to last past Monday.

So why, aside from the almost certain death of the lilacs, did she want to burst into tears?

"DON'T CRY."

"I can't help myself." She fished a tissue out of her pocket and wiped her eyes. "I thought you were dead."

"The shovel clipped me in the head, that's all." Patrick took the ice pack Kim fixed him and held it against the side of his head. He, Anna and the girls were assembled in the photo studio's reception room. Kate had insisted he lie down on the couch while Kim fixed the ice pack, but he felt silly. He wasn't dead yet, just temporarily out of commission.

"But you didn't answer when we talked to you," Kim said, so pale with worry that Patrick felt a pang of guilt.

"I turned my hearing aid off," he admitted. "The noise was giving me a headache, everyone talking all at once like that."

"The policemen were nice." Anna blew her nose and sniffed. "I don't think they wanted to arrest us."

"Arrest us?" Patrick snorted his disgust and sat up. "Jail two senior citizens in bad health? What kind of a story would that have been for the newspaper? Why, it would have looked like those men attacked us."

"It's all my fault," Anna sniffed. "I shouldn't have given out cookies instead of putting my handcuffs back on."

Patrick leaned over and patted her back. "It's not your fault that your cooking caused a small riot."

"That's not funny," she said. "They should have looked where they were going."

Kate walked over to the window that over-looked Lilac House. "Well, it's almost over. They've brought in a dump truck to haul the bushes away."

"I can't look," her twin said, and Patrick's heart ached at the look on Kimmy's face.

"It's best not to," he agreed.

"I hate to see things change." Kim said, wiping tears off her cheeks.

"Well, well, now," he said, his voice gruff. He never could stand to see women cry. "If I've learned anything in eighty-four years, it's that nothing stays the same. "

"Where'd Stuart go?" Kate asked the question the others didn't dare ask the weeping twin.

Kim shrugged. "Gone to work, I suppose."

"He should have stuck around," Patrick couldn't help pointing out. Her new boyfriend hadn't wasted any time bailing out when his fun weekend was over.

"No," Kim said, shaking her head. "When something's over, it's over."

Patrick readjusted his ice pack. He didn't like the sound of that one bit, but he could have told her days ago that Stuart fellow was not good enough for her.

HE WAS IN LOVE.

Painfully in love. Miserably in love. Pathetically in love. So of course he avoided calling

Kim. He didn't know what to say. *I'm afraid I'm in love with you? You scare the living hell right out of me? I don't know if I'm ready for babies and wedding rings and wall-to-wall carpet, but would you let me into your bed and let me make love to you three or four thousand times while I figure it out?*

Temple was no help, either. On her return from Mexico she listened to the whole story and told him she was sorry, but there was nothing she could do. Except advise that he either forget his baby photographer or marry her. And start planting lilacs. She'd be glad to tell him where he could buy plants and trees wholesale.

Payne called him four times a day—on his cell phone and by leaving messages at the hospital—to ask if he was serious about Kim and if that meant Brianne would have her growing years documented by a professional photographer? She said she liked the idea and was sure that Stuart's babies would be almost as beautiful as Brianne. And when, she wanted to know, was the wedding?

Wedding?

So on Friday night after work, Stuart decided to swing by the photo studio and drop off the bag Kim had left in his car. She'd miss the old bonnets and the Lobster Maine-ia sweatshirt. He hoped she wouldn't have had any reason to wear the black nightgown, but when he drove close to her place he saw Kim getting into a car, the door being held by an eager-looking man who looked way too pleased with himself.

Stuart wanted to ram the Mercedes into the front of that silver Mazda, but he'd never been the violent type. Still, it took all the control he possessed to keep his hands on the steering wheel. That guy had no business taking Kim out. She wore a short black dress and high-heeled black sandals, so this was no casual date. And she didn't look at all unhappy, as if she missed him.

He saw red. Literally red, as if all the blood had rushed to his eyeballs in a strange kind of rage.

So he pulled the car off to the side of the road and watched Kim and a guy who looked remotely like one of the construction workers drive down the street. And then he rested his forehead on the steering wheel and prayed that the man would never know the feel of Kim Cooper's silken thighs.

"You're too late," he heard a man say. When

he lifted his head and looked to the right he saw Kim's old neighbor, Pat O'Something, peering in his window. He pushed a button and the window rolled down.

"Yeah," Stuart said. "I guess I am."

"You look a little shook up, young man."

"I stopped by to bring her some things she left in my car."

"I see." Patrick motioned toward the ignition. "You'd better shut that fancy car of yours off and come inside. You look like you could use a drink."

"Yes, sir, I suppose I could." Though drinking with an ancient Irishman wasn't exactly what he'd planned to do this evening, the alternative was to go home to his empty condo and drown himself in self-pity while listening to his sisters' messages on his voice mail.

"Then come on, then."

So over a glass of exceptionally fine Irish whiskey, Stuart found himself pouring out his troubles to a man he barely knew. "I tried to buy Lilac House that morning," he confided. "But it's been sold as office condos to several businesses already. It was already too late by then to save the lilacs."

"You were going to buy the place for her?" the old man refilled their glasses. "Why?"

Stuart shrugged, unwilling to admit he wanted the woman with a ferocity that was almost embarrassing. "It seemed like a nice thing to do."

"A nice thing?" the man repeated. "That's all?"

"Well—"

"Do you love that woman or not?"

"I haven't had too much, uh, experience with that particular emotion," he confessed, wishing somehow this was a lot simpler.

"How'd you feel when you saw her with that other fella tonight?"

Stuart took a deep breath as he knew exactly what that man was thinking right now, over drinks or dinner. He would be trying to figure out how to get Kim into bed. "Not too good."

"Possessive-like?"

"In spades."

Patrick nodded. "That's what happens, son. When you can't stand the thought of her with anyone else, there's only one thing left to do."

"There is?" He had a feeling he knew what Patrick was getting at.

"Yep. But I hear you haven't called her,

didn't say goodbye, nothing. No nice words, even. Or flowers."

He couldn't defend himself. He was a real son of a bitch, all right. He took another sip of the whiskey and looked Patrick in the eye. "So what do I do now? Those damn bushes are gone and if I show up at her door with a bouquet of flowers she's likely to throw them in my face."

"Well, flowers and apologies are worth a shot, but I've got me another idea, one I've been kicking around all week. You want to hear it?"

Stuart Thorpe didn't want to hear anything else.

KIM THOUGHT ABOUT MOVING into the city to share Kate's apartment for a while. Every time she looked out the east window and saw the devastation that used to be her lilac garden, she felt her heart sink a little lower.

"Call him," Kate urged, helping her sort the latest batch of proofs. They often caught up with work and each other on Sunday afternoons and then went out for dinner. "He has your baby bonnets and your clothes. You ask him to drop them off."

"I can't. If Stuart wanted to see me or call me he would have by now."

"So the weekend was just a sexual fling."

"Yes."

"You don't have sexual flings."

"I do now," Kim insisted. "I'm a real flinger. A natural."

"And your date Friday night?"

"I wore the black dress and those shoes you gave me—which, by the way, gave me a blister on my little toe—and I got a headache and came home early."

"Alone?"

"Alone."

"Pining for the doctor."

"I don't pine," she fibbed, knowing damn well she'd given her heart to a man who rescued trombonists, comforted cranky babies and knew how to make love in a bathtub. But she had been foolish to think for a second he could have saved her lilacs. Foolish to think he was some kind of hero who would appear with the perfect solution: love, marriage and gardens ever after.

"Hmm," was her sister's only reply. They worked in uncustomary silence for a while longer, until Kate asked, "Did you get Anna's message?"

"No." Patrick and Anna hadn't been around

all weekend. There had been no invitation to Saturday's yard sales, no pot of meatballs, no anise cookies. Her neighbors were giving her time to mourn the lilacs, she supposed, but she missed their company. "What did she want?"

"They need help taking pictures of their latest eBay treasures."

"I'll call her and tell them to bring them over tomorrow. I'm pretty sure I'm free after four." She picked up the roll of film she'd used last weekend. It would have the pictures of Brianne and Stuart at Plymouth Rock.

"Whatever it is is too big, so she asked if you would come over to Patrick's house. I told her we'd come over around five."

"Today or tomorrow?" The film could wait a few more days. She was in no hurry to see the doctor's smiling eyes looking back at her.

"Today." Kate glanced at the clock. "Now would be okay, while the light is still good."

Kim stood and stretched. "Fine. Maybe afterward Anna will feed us."

"Yes," her twin said. "This could be our lucky day."

The street was quiet, the Lilac House workers having taken Sunday off. Kim saw that parts of the house sported new siding and windows, yet the architectural details had been left alone. Kim took her time crossing the lawn to Patrick's front porch, but Kate appeared to be in a hurry and reached the door before Kim.

"Hello!" she called through the screen. "Anybody home?"

Patrick, out of breath, appeared after a few moments.

"Hello, ladies," he panted. "We're out back. Come on in."

"Did we come at a bad time?"

"No. We've been waiting." He grinned at Kate and then held the door open so they could enter the foyer. Kim hadn't been in the house very often, but it was one of those solid older Victorians with high ceilings, wide trim and rooms that led on to rooms. A staircase was directly in front of them, and a long hall cut through the center of the house. He must be lonely, she thought, following him down the hall to the back door.

"What have you bought now?" she asked, trying to keep up with him. "It must be awfully big."

"It's not what I've bought," he said, pushing the back door open. "It's what I've sold."

"Sold?"

"Yep. I've sold the house."

Kim paused halfway out the door as Patrick waited for her on the brick patio. "What are you talking about?" She wanted to be happy for him, since he had such a large grin on his face, but she hated the idea of her old friend moving away. And what would Anna do?

"He'll tell you." Patrick jerked his thumb toward the far corner of the yard and Kim's gaze landed on the sight of Stuart Thorpe leaning on a shovel. He wore jeans and a dirt-spattered denim shirt, its sleeves rolled up past his wrists.

"What are you doing here?" was all she could think to ask.

"Planting," he said. "Want to see?" He came toward her and held out his hand. She took it automatically and he led her toward a scraggly row of lilac bushes.

"Lilacs?"

"For you," he declared. "Patrick and I have been planting for two days." She looked past him and realized that a corner of the large backyard was blocked by lilac bushes. "I know they're not what you're used to, but they'll grow. The nursery assured me they would."

"Patrick said he sold the house." She turned back to Stuart and tried to figure out what was going on here. Her fingers stayed tucked snugly inside his hand.

"To me," he declared. "On one condition."

"What?"

"That you live here, too."

Kim stared up at him.

"I couldn't buy Lilac House for you," he continued. "And I'm sorry I couldn't save the lilacs. I tried, but it was too late. When I saw that my sister's business was the owner, I called her—"

"Your *sister*?"

"Temple. She *is* New England Renovation. Has been for ten years. She says she likes having all those men at her beck and call. That's why I left so fast on Tuesday—but she'd already sold three of the office units and couldn't cancel the deals, so—"

"You bought Patrick's house instead?"

"Yes. It was his idea."

"You already have a house," she pointed out. "In Newport."

"Temple is going to buy it. Please don't frown at me like that," he said. "You're supposed to fall into my arms and say yes."

"Say yes to what?"

"To marrying me. To becoming Auntie Kim.

To helping me spread fertilizer on the lilacs 'til death do us part." He tugged her hand to his lips and kissed her knuckles. "Come on, sweetheart. Give me a break."

She looked over her shoulder, but Patrick and Kate had disappeared. No doubt they, along with Anna, were watching from one of the windows. Stuart pulled her gently inside the new lilac garden, which would someday be as private and gorgeous as the one Lilac House possessed.

"Say something," he said, cradling her face with his hands. He smelled of dirt and lilacs. "Say you'll marry me."

"Say you love me," she whispered, wondering if her heart could pound any faster.

"I do. Very much. Love you," he said, punctuating his words with small kisses on her mouth. "I've been falling at your feet since I saw you last week. Haven't you noticed?"

She looped her arms around his waist. "No. I was too busy falling in love and trying to hide it."

"Is that a 'yes I'll marry you Stuart' answer?"

"Yes, but—"

He frowned. "But what?"

"The honeymoon," she whispered, lifting her

mouth to his. "Does it have to be at a histori- cally significant place?"

Stuart's eyebrows rose. "I had my heart set on John Adams's birthplace."

Kim pretended to think that over. "All right," she conceded. "As long as next time your niece stays home."

He paused, his thumbs brushing her mouth. "If you'll promise to marry me, I will take you anywhere and everywhere you want to go. With or without babies."

"You have a deal," she told him, and kissed the man she loved as the scent of lilacs sur- rounded them.

"HOW ABOUT SOME SUPPER?" Anna wiped tears from her eyes and poked Patrick's arm. "We need to leave the young folks alone."

"Fine." He'd worked up quite an appetite with all that gardening.

"Come on, Kate," Anna said. "Let's go over to my house and pour some wine to celebrate."

Kate took another look out the window. "They're still kissing," she said. "I think that's a good sign."

Patrick agreed. "That young man will do just

fine. He and Kimmy will have a good life in this house, just like my Mary and me did."

"But where are you going to live? With your daughter?"

"Nope." He patted Kate's shoulder and turned her toward the kitchen door and Anna's house. "Anna's converting her second floor into an apartment and I'm going to rent it."

"I can't do stairs anymore," the old woman confessed. She turned toward Kate. "I think I'd feel safer with a man living upstairs." She stopped to peer out the window over the sink. "They're still together out there."

"That's perfect," Kate told them. "I'm glad you're not moving away, Patrick."

"And leave Anna's cooking? Never." The women laughed, thinking he was joking.

"I'd hate to think you would miss the wedding."

"Ooh," Anna said. "The *wedding!* Oh, my, won't that be a day!"

Patrick ushered them out the door and into the driveway before they could start talking about dresses and flowers and all those things. He grinned and peeked around the corner of the house to see the young couple in each other's arms. "What are we having for supper, Anna?"

"I made a nice lasagna while you were busy with the lilacs."

He didn't know who was the luckiest man, him or Stuart, but when he followed Anna across the yard Patrick decided that Kimmy's babies were certain to have reddish-gold hair.

HARLEQUIN®

Temptation

THE WRONG BED

What happens when a girl finds herself in the
wrong bed...with the *right* guy?

Find out in:

#866 NAUGHTY BY NATURE by Jule McBride
February 2002

#870 SOMETHING WILD by Toni Blake
March 2002

#874 CARRIED AWAY by Donna Kauffman
April 2002

#878 HER PERFECT STRANGER by Jill Shalvis
May 2002

#882 BARELY MISTAKEN by Jennifer LaBrecque
June 2002

#886 TWO TO TANGLE by Leslie Kelly
July 2002

Midnight mix-ups have never been so much fun!

HARLEQUIN®
Makes any time special®

Visit us at www.eHarlequin.com

HTNBN2

HARLEQUIN®
Temptation.

Look for bed, breakfast and more...!

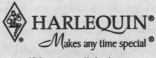
COOPER'S CORNER

Some of your favorite Temptation authors are checking in early at Cooper's Corner Bed and Breakfast

In May 2002:

**#877 *The Baby and the Bachelor*
Kristine Rolofson**

In June 2002:

**#881 *Double Exposure*
Vicki Lewis Thompson**

In July 2002:

**#885 *For the Love of Nick*
Jill Shalvis**

In August 2002 things heat up even more at Cooper's Corner. There's a whole year of intrigue and excitement to come—twelve fabulous books bound to capture your heart and mind!

Join all your favorite Harlequin authors in Cooper's Corner!

HARLEQUIN®
Makes any time special ®

Visit us at www.eHarlequin.com

HTCC

If you enjoyed what you just read,
then we've got an offer you can't resist!

Take 2 bestselling love stories FREE!

Plus get a FREE surprise gift!

Clip this page and mail it to Harlequin Reader Service®

IN U.S.A.	IN CANADA
3010 Walden Ave.	P.O. Box 609
P.O. Box 1867	Fort Erie, Ontario
Buffalo, N.Y. 14240-1867	L2A 5X3

YES! Please send me 2 free Harlequin Temptation® novels and my free surprise gift. After receiving them, if I don't wish to receive anymore, I can return the shipping statement marked cancel. If I don't cancel, I will receive 4 brand-new novels each month, before they're available in stores. In the U.S.A., bill me at the bargain price of $3.34 plus 25¢ shipping and handling per book and applicable sales tax, if any*. In Canada, bill me at the bargain price of $3.80 plus 25¢ shipping and handling per book and applicable taxes**. That's the complete price and a savings of 10% off the cover prices—what a great deal! I understand that accepting the 2 free books and gift places me under no obligation ever to buy any books. I can always return a shipment and cancel at any time. Even if I never buy another book from Harlequin, the 2 free books and gift are mine to keep forever.

142 HEN DFND
342 HEN DFNE

Name	(PLEASE PRINT)	
Address	Apt.#	
City	State/Prov.	Zip/Postal Code

* Terms and prices subject to change without notice. Sales tax applicable in N.Y.
** Canadian residents will be charged applicable provincial taxes and GST.
  All orders subject to approval. Offer limited to one per household and not valid to
  current Harlequin Temptation® subscribers.
  ® are registered trademarks of Harlequin Enterprises Limited.

TEMP01   ©1998 Harlequin Enterprises Limited

eHARLEQUIN.com

| community | membership |

| buy books | authors | online reads | magazine | learn to write |

buy books

Your one-stop shop for great reads at great prices.
We have all your favorite Harlequin, Silhouette,
MIRA and Steeple Hill books, as well as a host of
other bestsellers in Other Romances. Discover a
wide array of new releases, bargains and hard-to-
find books today!

learn to write

Become the writer you always knew you could be:
get tips and tools on how to craft the perfect
romance novel and have your work critiqued by
professional experts in romance fiction. Follow
your dream now!

HARLEQUIN®

Makes any time special®—online...

Visit us at
www.eHarlequin.com

HINTLTW

HARLEQUIN®
Temptation.

It's hot...and it's out of control!

This spring, the forecast is hot and steamy!
Don't miss these bold, provocative, ultra-sexy books!

PRIVATE INVESTIGATIONS by Tori Carrington
April 2002
Secretary-turned-P.I. Ripley Logan never thought her first job
would have her running for her life—or crawling into
a stranger's bed....

ONE HOT NUMBER by Sandy Steen
May 2002
Accountant Samantha Collins may be good with numbers, but
she needs some work with men...until she meets sexy but
broke rancher Ryder Wells. Then she decides to make him a
deal—her brains for his bed. Sam's getting the better of the
deal, but hey, who's counting?

WHAT'S YOUR PLEASURE? by Julie Elizabeth Leto
June 2002
Mystery writer Devon Michaels is in a bind. Her publisher has
promised her a lucrative contract, *if* she makes the jump to
erotic thrillers. The problem: Devon can't write a love scene to
save her life. Luckily for her, Detective Jake Tanner is an
expert at "hands-on" training....

Don't miss this thrilling threesome!

HARLEQUIN®
Makes any time special ®

Visit us at www.eHarlequin.com

HTH